DATE DUE JUN 0 6

GAYLORD			PRINTED IN U.S.A.

A GUIDING STAR

A GUIDING STAR

Joyce Stranger

This first world edition published in Great Britain 2006 by
SEVERN HOUSE PUBLISHERS LTD of
9–15 High Street, Sutton, Surrey SM1 1DF.
This first world edition published in the USA 2006 by
SEVERN HOUSE PUBLISHERS INC of
595 Madison Avenue, New York, N.Y. 10022.

British Library Cataloguing in Publication Data

Stranger, Joyce
   A guiding star
   1.   Widows - Fiction
   2.   Traffic accident victims - Fiction
   3.   Human-animal relationships - Fiction
   4.   Highlands (Scotland) - Fiction
   I.   Title
   823.9'14 [F]

   ISBN-13: 978-0-7278-6364-5
   ISBN-10: 0-7278-6364-9

Typeset by Palimpsest Book Production Ltd.,
Polmont, Stirlingshire, Scotland.
Printed and bound in Great Britain by
MPG Books Ltd., Bodmin, Cornwall.

This book is dedicated to Harry Watson, who has been my editor and my own guiding star throughout its initial writing, as it began its life as a serial for *My Weekly* Magazine.

He has helped me make it into a far better story.

Thank you, Harry.

One

The Golden Retriever was alone for the first time in her short life. No one to feed her, comfort her, tend her. No safety, anywhere. She was out on the hills in a place she had never seen before. She was two years old and up to now had been cherished. Within minutes, her life had changed. Rain soaked her thick fur. Her paws, unused to running over stony ground, were sore. She had no knowledge to help her. Only instinct. Instinct told her she must hide. Instinct told her she must be wary. Instinct told her she could no longer trust.

There was nothing familiar anywhere. She was in a wilderness. No houses. No people. She was cold. She was used to a warm house and a warm bed, to food being given her. Now she had to find her own food, or starve.

She needed to find her way home, back to the people who had loved her, but she could not do that yet. She sensed that it was far away. There was not even a hint of home on the air. The wind that swept down the mountains chilled her. February this year was pitiless.

Her pups were almost due. Another few days and they would be born. Her bulk hampered her, but she dare not stop. Behind was fear. She had never before been out alone in the dark. She had led a sheltered life. Now she was lost. She wanted her home. She wanted her owners. She had never been so hungry.

She lay in the shelter of a bush, trying to evade the driving rain. She lay curled, nose on her paws. Remembering.

She remembered warmth. She remembered her bed, with its soft rug. It was sanctuary, where she could curl up and be safe. She remembered the hand that stretched to stroke her just before the lights went out at night. Her master and mistress too were preparing for sleep in the big bed that

1

overshadowed her small one. She remembered the voices that said 'Goodnight, Star.' She loved them both so much. She ached with loneliness and longing for them.

Why had she been snatched from her home and brought to this lonely place? She could not understand. The men had hurt her. They had flung her on to smelly straw and driven through the night. When they tried to get her out of the van they had kicked her. She felt ill from the drug they had given her, but terror inspired her.

She retaliated and bit one of them and escaped. She had run as she had never run before, hiding from their shouting voices and the sticks that thrashed the undergrowth, trying to find her. Now she knew that humans were not always kind. For the first time in her life she lived with fear.

The desire for life dominated her. Life for her and for the pups growing inside her. It was her first litter and she was as yet unaware of the reasons for the changes in her body. Instinct came to her aid. Instinct to preserve herself. Instinct to preserve her young. Instinct to find shelter and food. Instinct to live as her wild ancestors had lived long ago.

She had not had a wild mother to teach her. She was disadvantaged. Every creature around her had been born to this wilderness and knew how to survive, having been taught from its earliest days. She did not know the tricks and wiles that ensured that she too would survive. She did not know the safe trails that would keep her from enemies, whether human or animal. She had never been forced to sleep in the rain before or find her own sanctuary.

Her owners had ensured that she was strong and healthy. She had to learn to find warmth and food. She had to ensure that she and her young thrived. She had to teach herself new skills. She had to develop cunning. The need to survive was paramount.

When day came she ran until she could run no more. There was only the vast expanse of heath and heather, and high above her a circling bird with giant wings, looking down on her. His shadow crossed the ground. He had seen easier prey. The Retriever was large and the eagle did not know that she was unskilled in fighting.

She moved into deep cover, and the threat passed.

She had often walked in woods, but they were small and friendly places and she had not been alone. She knew the smells of animals she had been forbidden to chase. Rabbit scent lay heavily on the ground. Also that of hares and deer.

The mountains rose above her, towering into the sky. Below her in the valley cars raced along the roads. She knew about those. They meant danger. On those walks that she had so loved she had been told to sit when she came to a kerb. Told to wait until the road was clear and not a single vehicle in sight before they crossed. Told by the people who to her were more important than anything else in her life. If only they were there to bring her food. She was so hungry.

She heard their voices in her memory.

'Star, find Liz.'

'Star, find Matt.'

She loved looking for them, nudging them, telling each of them that the other partner wanted them. They laughed when she found them and hugged her. She adored both of them, but Matt meant most to her. She greeted him with her whole body in ecstatic motion and a wildly waving tail, delighted always to see him.

Liz gave her food and cuddled her. Matt walked with her and taught her. She ached for them with a deep need, and whimpered softly to herself, longing for their company.

She always knew a moment of panic if Matt was out of sight among the trees, and then came his voice, reassuring her, claiming her.

'Star, come, Star. Where are you? Come, girl.'

She would stop, electrified, her eyes looking for him. She raced to find him, and leaned against him, eager for the caressing hand and the voice that told her she had done well.

'Good girl. What a star.'

Star. She knew her name.

She thought of them and dreamed of them. She needed to find them again.

For a few moments her tail beat against the ground as she remembered. She could almost hear Matt's voice, and her ears pricked eagerly. The memory faded and there was only the wind hurling itself against the trees. The branches bent and twisted and she thought that they cried in agony, sharing her desolation.

She hated wind. She never could understand why she couldn't see it. It was an invisible creature that ruffled her fur and tonight blew rain into her face. She turned and curled up, nose to tail, but she had little shelter.

She longed to hear Matt. Surely he would be near, looking for her, would call to her as he always did, summoning her to him, to home, to safety. Or maybe Liz would look for her. Life had been such fun. Now everything she knew had gone.

Surely they would never leave her out in the wild, alone. She listened but the only sounds were those of the trees responding to the rising gale, and the whisper of rain on the mossy ground. There were clouds in the sky above her, dark clouds that ran before the wind.

Memories filled her mind. She moved again, striving to get comfortable enough to rest. This time she lay with her nose on her paws, whimpering very softly to herself, hidden under dense bramble cover, her eyes staring into a past that had vanished.

Where had they gone and why had she been brought here?

She huddled even closer, and fell into an uneasy sleep, dreaming of the past while the wind rose and hammered the trees and the wilderness closed round her. She woke, cold, hungry and terrified.

Two

It had been a tough day. It was cold and, according to the weather pundits, the wettest March in that part of the Scottish Highlands for nearly a hundred years. Greg McLeod was so tired. He needed more help on the farm. He needed sleep. His lambing ewes always seemed to have problems at night. Those born during the day popped out without any trouble. It was two weeks since he had spent a whole night in his bed.

His legs ached. He was cold and he was hungry. He tried to shrug off the misery he felt. His mood would lift once he was safe and warm again.

Nothing had gone right for the past year. Greg felt angry whenever he thought of the day that had so changed life for himself and his wife and his daughter and her little son.

The only consolation was the huge insurance that had paid for alterations to the farmhouse for Shelley's wheelchair and was paying for the new bungalow that Greg began to think would never be finished. It would be better for all of them for Shelley and Dannie to have a place on their own.

Dannie had been playing up when Greg left to look over the sheep. Lambing time was always busy and a small boy intent on mischief as a result of anger did not help. Dannie did not like the animals. He was a determined child, and when he set his heart on something pestered until every adult around him wanted to shake him.

Greg was tired. He sat on the top of the low wall beside the path and his sheepdog Meg came to lean against him. He needed to rest, and rest was rarely possible if Dannie were around. His thoughts milled.

Greg wished he could forget the day that the police had informed them that David, their son in law, had been killed in a road accident and their daughter, Shelley, very badly injured.

The memories returned, unwanted. The accident had changed life for so many people. He could not leave the farm as they had no help now and though friends did help when they heard the news, they could not take over. Sheina, his wife, had flown to London. Dannie, then five, had been at home with a babysitter, a neighbour girl named Christine whose mother cared for him until Sheina arrived to bring him back to the farm.

David, Greg's son-in-law, had not been born till his mother was over forty and his parents were much older than Greg and Sheina and felt unable to cope with a small child. It might have been better for Dannie if there had been a grave to visit but David's parents had lost their only child. They insisted their son was buried in his home village, far away in the south of England, at the church they had all attended when he was a boy and where his grandparents lay in the family plot.

On that dreadful day Shelley and David had gone out for a birthday celebration.

They crashed on their way home. Police investigation proved that David was well over the limit for driving after drinking. He had insisted that he was below it. Shelley had believed him, not knowing that while she was in the cloak-room he had increased the effect of the wine they had drunk with a double whisky.

If only Shelley had stayed at home and married a local man. As it was, she met David while away in college and they married as soon as they had their degrees. Shelley had gone on to design fabrics for an elegant fashion house in London; a job that kept her far away from her parents. It had been impossible for Greg and Sheina to leave their home to visit them and their only contact over the next few years had been the young couple's flying visits to the farm, during which Greg and his wife barely got to know their little grandson. Dannie had not liked the farm on his visits and he still did not. He was afraid of the animals. He wanted to be at home with his computer games and for some strange reason he kept asking to go to the supermarket.

Shelley, when told about this, had laughed.

'They have this little automatic car he can ride in, outside the store,' she said. 'I always let him have a ride in it if he's been good.'

Greg eased himself, but felt reluctant to leave his perch. He looked down on the farm, so many feet below him. The steep downward path made his knees ache. Going up wasn't so bad. Meg waved her tail uncertainly, wondering why they did not continue home. She was hungry.

Greg wanted to think about Dannie. Perhaps there was some way he could treat him tonight that would help the child accept his mother. He seemed to reject her now she was home. There must be some way they could help the child. He was a very confused and unhappy little boy.

Greg had so looked forward to having grandchildren. Grandchildren to teach about the farm, to share his passion for his animals. To take to the pony club, as they had taken Shelley. She had been a local star, her sights set on a showjumping career.

It hurt him so much to see her now. She had been such an active child, running everywhere, full of life and laughter, racing in from school, saddling up her pony, out in the field practising over the jumps he had made. Off to play tennis, or to walk on the hills with her friends, or to take one of the dogs out to practise herding for the sheepdog trials.

She made friends so easily, which was good as for some reason there were no brothers or sisters. They just didn't happen.

There had been two men working on the farm then, and he and Sheina had been free to take her to various shows, enjoying the day out, meeting friends and vying happily over their children's prowess.

Even if he did ever get Dannie interested in riding, there was no chance now of taking days off. It was impossible to get anyone to stay long in such an out-of-the-way place. The village boys all left. Farming did not appeal to them, and they looked for far better paid work in the towns and cities. And it didn't seem likely. Dannie spent hours in his room playing with his computer, but showed little interest in physical activities. He appeared to have inherited none of his

7

mother's coordination, turning up with bruises so often that Greg could only conclude that Shelley's former grace had died with the accident, never to be reborn in her clumsy son. Even if Dannie wasn't always bumping into things, he had never shown any pleasure in the horses.

They ought perhaps to sell the farm, but he did not want to retire. The animals were his life, and Sheina's. The day would come, but not now.

The doctors had told Shelley it was most unlikely that she would walk again. The physiotherapist who came twice a week was more hopeful , insisting that if she made the effort, she would be able to move around, although in a limited fashion. She had begun her treatment while in hospital, but since she came home she seemed to be overwhelmed all over again with grief for David, and her moods fluctuated wildly between half-acceptance and despair.

Dannie made matters worse, as he was sure that his mother could walk if she wanted. She had been in the hospital for almost a year and only come home a month ago. Ever since she and Dannie seemed to be at war. No matter how hard his mother tried, he did his best to do the opposite of everything she asked of him.

Greg wondered if he ought to be more severe, but the child was so small. And so determined. The sudden change in his life had been an enormous shock. And he and his father had adored each other. Greg wondered at times if they would ever get back to normal.

Shelley had always been independent and she insisted now on doing as much as she could, but railed at the fact that she was so limited. Although she and Dannie had their own rooms and bathroom downstairs, they always ate with Greg and Sheina. Shelley prepared vegetables and cooked their meals, freeing her mother for other jobs around the farm. She was only disabled from the waist down. Her back had been badly injured but she could use her arms.

She was still in a great deal of pain and on the bad days despair dominated her. She tried not to burden her parents with her fears, but they knew how she felt.

'She's cutting herself off from all her friends,' Sheina had said the night before, after Shelley had gone to bed. 'She thinks they pity her and people who don't know her tend to treat her as if she had lost her wits as well as the use of her legs.'

'People just don't know quite how to behave round her,' he had answered. 'Give her time.'

He wondered if his daughter felt as bitter about her husband as he did. Only one mistake. But in his view it was unforgivable. It had never happened before, Shelley said. It had been a special day, with a promotion to celebrate as well as a birthday.

David was to be manager of the Midlands branch of his firm. They would be nearer and might be able to visit more often. They had both been excited by the prospect, toasting their future. Maybe David had got careless after those first glasses of wine. Maybe Shelley too had had her judgement impaired, as she was probably not fit to drive.

She refused to talk about the accident. Was it better to make her remember, or would that make things worse? She had been offered counselling but had refused it, saying it wouldn't help.

If only they had taken a taxi. But it was no use trying to reshape the past. They had to live with the present.

He pushed the unwanted thoughts out of his head.

The hoped-for spring warmth hadn't come. He did not want to leave the lambs to lie in frosty fields. They and their mothers were in the barns, causing more work than ever. There were more ewes on the hills, their lambs as yet unborn. Hopefully they would not need to come in until those in the barn were old enough to risk the frosty nights outside. He sighed and stood up. Time to get on.

Sheina was walking across the yard towards him as he discarded his wet clothing in the porch. Lights shone from the windows. The alterations made their home seem an alien place. It had been in the family for five generations, and was old when the young Victoria came to the throne.

It was now modernized. The outside steps had been replaced with a ramp, and all the doorways widened to accommodate the wheelchair. It had made for disruption and only just been completed in time for Shelley to come home.

Greg looked down at his side, feeling a weight against his

legs. Twelve-year-old Meg was also exhausted. She collapsed against him. He lifted her and held her briefly, wishing she were young again. She was losing weight. He sighed, hating old age whether in humans or animals.

Meg was really too old for the job but his young dog, Rab, had a badly cut paw, and was only able to limp on three legs. Sheina opened the kitchen door for him and warm air flooded out. When Greg put the collie down again she greeted her mistress wearily with a token tail wag.

'Bad day?' they both asked together and then laughed.

'Just the usual sheep day, and the foul weather,' Greg said. 'We had to hunt for one of the ewes and her lamb. Old Trouble. Wouldn't you know it? She'd wandered off and I suspect her lamb, who's as bad as she is, forded the river on to a bank. She followed and then rain caused the water to rise and she and the lamb were cut off.'

'I hope you didn't swim for it,' his wife said.

He dropped into his big armchair and wrestled with his boots.

'It wasn't that deep. Silly beast panicked. I carried her lamb and she followed without a problem. Shelley and Dannie OK?'

The door opened and Shelley came in.

'Hi, Dad. You look frozen.' She wheeled herself to the Aga and poured hot water into a mug that was standing ready. 'It's not been the best of days, has it, Mum? Dannie's in one of his worse moods.'

She sighed as Greg took the mug from her and cupped his hands round it, savouring the heat.

'I sometimes feel he hates me.'

'Of course he doesn't,' Sheina said as she bent to give Meg a bowl of food.

'Where is he?' Greg asked. 'Ought I to go to him?'

'He's playing one of his horrible computer games. Zap, zap, you're dead. I told David not to give them to him. Killing and gore. If I take them from him he shouts at me and yesterday he kicked me. I didn't want David to buy them. I don't like all this violence and I'm sure it's bad for children. But he always said boys will be boys and it would get it out of his system.'

'He'd be better off with games that teach him how it feels to drive,' Greg said. 'I'm sure there are some. The kind they use in driving schools. As if you were driving yourself, with the road unwinding before you and odd incidents cropping up. That would surely be fun. And it's probably a good idea after everything that's happened that he doesn't grow up scared of cars. Maybe I can find one when I next go to town. I haven't liked to take the others away from him. They're his only memories of his father.'

'He won't talk about David. And I don't know how I feel. There are days when I hate him, because of the accident. But I loved him . . . he was great fun, and it was a very happy marriage.'

She turned her wheelchair so that her parents couldn't see her tears.

The door swung shut behind her. Greg stared at the blank wood. Sheina sighed, wishing she could wave a wand and right the world.

'I feel so helpless,' she said.

'That makes two of us.'

Greg slumped into the battered armchair beside the Aga. Outside the rising gale keened as if Dannie's imagined banshees were wailing to the sky. He could not be persuaded it was only the wind whining round the corners. Sheina thought she heard a distant dog howling, a lonely noise in the dark, but the sound died away as Greg drew his chair nearer to the fire. She watched him in quiet concern as he shivered.

'Another coffee?'

Greg nodded.

There was always a kettle sitting on the Aga ready for use. Sheina poured boiling water on to instant coffee, added milk and brought one of the mugs across to Greg. She perched on the bench beside the pine table.

'Dannie's steadily getting more and more impossible. He brought a long letter from his Head today . . . or whatever they call her these days.'

Greg laughed, but he didn't sound amused.

'Probably a Human Resources Manager or some such,' he said. 'Are we behind the times or just plain sensible? What's Dannie done now?'

11

'She says that the school would like him referred to a psychologist. He may need a special school. He's increasingly disruptive, bullying smaller children and breaking their toys and pencils. He took one child's glasses off and stamped on them and broke them. The little girl hates wearing them and it's made matters worse. Shelley can't cope . . . and for that matter I'm beginning to have problems too. When he came home today he wouldn't do a thing we asked of him.'

'I wonder . . .'Greg said.

He had been listening with increasing dismay. He wanted to push the thought away but it intruded. Sheina was slicing meat from a joint of cold lamb. Baked jacket potatoes were in the Aga. She strained the beans.

'Last of our own. I'll have to go to the supermarket and stock up on vegetables. Be a while before we get any here. What do you wonder?'

'There isn't a special school anywhere near here. Are they residential? Suppose they take him away from us?'

The thought was more than either of them could bear.

Three

Peace did not last long. Greg was settling down wearily to a meal Sheina placed before him when raised voices from the annexe grew more and more shrill. A door slammed. There was a patter of footsteps outside the door. It was flung open and Dannie erupted into the room.

His anorak was round his shoulders, his usually blonde hair coloured a curious pink. The jersey that had been clean when he went to his own room was discoloured with some substance they could not identify.

'I wanted my hair to look like that man on the telly and like the girl in the post office,' Dannie shouted. The two dogs hastily left the room to lie in the barn where the orphan lambs were in pens. 'Mummy didn't have anything I could use to do it so I used the cooking fat. And cochineal. I took it out of the cupboard when you were feeding the chickens. And Mummy got mad at me and so I comed here.'

He stared up at his grandparents, who were both temporarily speechless. The postmistress's daughter was sixteen and had recently left school. She occasionally helped her mother. Her unconventional clothes and spiky scarlet hairstyle shocked most of the village.

'Mummy yelled at me to get out while she cleared up the mess. It wasn't much mess only I did spill it in the wash basin and on the floor.'

Greg went into the annexe where his infuriated daughter shouted at him.

'Dannie's determined to make everyone's life hell. I can't cope with him. I don't know what to do with him. And stop running around after me. I can manage. I'm not completely useless. I do have arms.'

Greg sighed. It was so hard for her. Cleaning up was not

easy when in a wheelchair but Shelley insisted on being as independent as possible, which was surely good, but did make life hard for those around her at times. She resented people who thought her unable to cope.

He went back to the kitchen where Sheina was trying to quieten Dannie.

'I don't want to be bathed. I want my hair to look like this when I go to school tomorrow. Paul said I wouldn't dare so I just showed him. He won't see it if it washes out.'

'Suppose we try something less messy afterwards,' Sheina said, hoping that by morning this particular fad would be forgotten. Maybe she could give a less startling imitation of the effect he desired. 'Grandad might have some hair cream. Who's Paul?'

Dannie was remarkably quiet about his time at school, but tonight his anger made him ready to talk. His mother was always yelling at him. It wasn't fair.

'He's my best friend. He's a year older than me only he's in our class too 'cos he didn't do that well last year. He came the same day as I did. They only just moved. He used to live in London too only not near us. He knows everything. And he can spit right across the room. I can only spit halfway. Shall I show you?'

'Nice people don't spit,' Sheina said.

'Paul does and he's nice,' Dannie shouted at her. 'He's nicer than you and nicer than Grandad and nicer than Mummy and he knows lots and lots of things.'

'Would you like a jacket potato?' Sheina asked, not anxious to pursue that line of conversation.

'I want chips.'

'You could try saying "Please,"' Sheina had spent much of the late afternoon with Dannie, who had come home from school in an even worse temper than usual. 'What you want, my little lad, is a firm hand and a bath and I'm giving it to you.'

'I'll bathe him,' Greg said. He had his own methods of dealing with this small tearaway.

He picked his grandson up and carried him upstairs, his shouts of protest causing the dogs to bark. Sheina put the potatoes back in the oven and the green beans on a plate

14

over a saucepan of boiling water to keep warm. It wasn't the first time Dannie had disrupted their evening. There were, she thought, disadvantages in having a grandson living with them.

He had been far worse since his mother came home.

His grandfather ignored shouts and yells and stamps. Dannie refused to be helpful in any way so Greg undressed him silently after managing to uncross his arms. He was lifted and dumped in the bath. Sheep were easier to dip, his grandfather thought as he scrubbed the colour and fat out of the child's hair. They at least could not argue even though they might fight him. Greg cleaned Dannie thoroughly, and also washed his hair until there was not a trace of cooking fat.

'I hate you.'

Dannie sat on the top stair and refused to move. He was carried downstairs, sat on the bench, and a jacket potato put in front of him.

'I want chips,' Dannie said, but in a far less demanding voice than before.

'I haven't any,' Sheina said. 'Eat up like a good boy.'

She bent over him and hugged him.

'You can be such a lovely boy,' she said. 'Why don't you try and show Mummy how good you really are?'

'Paul doesn't like goody-goodies. So they have to pay for it.'

'Pay for being good?' Greg looked at his grandson, startled, and wondering just what was going on at school when Paul and Dannie were together.

'Yes. He says only stupid people are good. Clever people can think up all sorts of things to do. The rest are good because they can't think, so just do as they're told all the time. Like sheep. The clever ones come from another planet, so they aren't really like other people at all. Paul says he and I come from the aliens. When we were babies they put us in the cots and took the real babies away.'

Greg looked at his wife, wondering just how they were going to disillusion the child.

'It's a secret. I wasn't supposed to tell you. When we grow up we'll take over the whole world and get rid of all the goody-goodies. It's all in this book Paul's dad gave him. Only I can't read it all yet. It's too difficult.'

Sheina added baked beans to the jacket potato. They were always a favourite with Dannie. He had had one meal already, but seemed to be able to eat at any time of day, and put away more than she thought possible. In spite of that he was a skinny child. Hollow legs, her grandmother would have said.

Maybe he would settle now, Sheina thought. He was much quieter.

'Like to go to bed and I'll tell you a story?' she asked, looking at the green beans on the side of his plate, untouched.

'What about?'

'A little bull that would never eat up his cabbage and wouldn't grow. And then he found a different kind of cabbage and couldn't stop eating it, and he grew into a prize-winning bull.'

'Tell me here. I don't want to go to bed.'

Greg looked at the child and grinned.

'I bet you a pound you can't get undressed and into bed before Gran counts one hundred.'

'I can so,' Dannie shouted and was out of his chair and into their part of the house before Greg had even stood up from his chair.

Sheina followed her grandson, wondering if that had been a good idea. It established a precedent. On the other hand, it did get the behaviour they wanted. She raised one eyebrow as she passed her husband and he grinned at her and whispered, 'Bribery will get you anything.'

Not a good idea, Sheina concluded as she went into the child's bedroom. But how on earth did they cope with the situation?

Greg collected the used dishes to stack in the dishwasher. He wished that life did not throw up so many problems. Children got the most extraordinary notions, but this boy beat them all. It had surely been easier when Shelley was Dannie's age. He and Sheina had been much younger then.

And his daughter hadn't lost her father and had to learn to live with a crippled mother.

How were they going to persuade Dannie that his ideas of aliens were absolute nonsense? Greg had a sudden memory

16

of a day when he was six years old. He had committed some childish peccadillo. He couldn't even remember what that was now. What he did remember was being sent up to his room until he apologized. He sat on his bed hating his parents and decided the real truth was that he was adopted and they hadn't told him. Probably he had someone aristocratic for a father, like an earl or something, and a film star for a mother who didn't want a baby because she was so busy being famous.

How long had he thought that, Greg wondered. He couldn't remember when he stopped using such thoughts to comfort himself when he was naughty. He was always sent to his room until he apologized. Often his grandfather, who lived with them, came upstairs and sat on the bed with him, smoking his pipe, and saying nothing much.

'Apologies never hurt anyone,' he used to say. 'We all make mistakes. That's the way we learn.'

Greg hoped Dannie would remember him with as much affection as he remembered his own grandfather. The smell of tweed and pipe smoke had been oddly comforting.

He sat in his big armchair and stroked the two dogs. His father would be turning in his grave, he thought. No sheep-dogs in the house in his own young days. Sheina had other ideas. She was too soft, he sometimes thought, for a farmer's wife. She fought to save any sick animal and only gave up when the vet told her they could do nothing more. He sighed. But he wouldn't have her different.

He switched on the television set but was sound asleep when his wife returned.

'I know it's daft,' she said, as she shook him gently. 'But you have to wake up and go to bed!'

'Dannie settle?'

'Yes. He went to sleep before I'd finished my story. Greg, what are we going to do about him? Shelley's getting desperate. I think that I am, too.'

Greg had no answer for her.

17

Four

Up on the hill high above the farmhouse, Star found a sitting hen, escaped from a farmyard. All old inhibitions vanished. She had only one need and that was to stay alive. The hen and her twelve eggs provided an ample meal. The birth was imminent and although Star did not know what was happening to her, instinct told her to find a place to lie in safety, a place where no one could find her. Later that day a hiker passed near her, pack on his back, heavy boots thumping the ground.

She fled at the sound. She no longer trusted strangers. He was unaware of her, hiding among the bushes, her eyes watching him.

She was hungry again, and thirsty. There was no food but there were pools on the ground where she could slake her thirst. She heard movement in the woods. The hiker had stopped to eat. When he left she found an uneaten sandwich thrown on the grass. He had left it for the birds. She devoured it. It was not nearly enough.

Movement triggered the birth pangs. She had no time to hunt. She needed shelter. She struggled upwards, sensing this led her away from danger. Every boulder was an obstacle. The stony ground hurt her pads. She found sanctuary at last among cluster of rocks that formed an overhang and kept out the worst of the weather. The ground was soft with moss.

By the time she settled the wind had dropped and the rain ceased. A thin new moon played hide and seek among the scattered clouds. Voices sounded below her as two young men passed by. They intended to climb the most challenging face of the mountain, tempted by a calm night, and restless with youth and energy.

The voices died away but she did not feel safe. Her rest

had given her new strength. She left the shelter of the trees. Her progress was blocked by a drystone wall which normally she would have cleared with ease, but her burden of pups made that impossible.

She smelled sheep. She was used to those. Though she was not bred to it, Matt had taught her to herd his tiny flock, and his sheep were her friends. She slept beside them, and played with the lambs. These sheep were in no danger from her.

Long-ago instincts drove her, telling her what she needed to do. Pain needled, and she walked clumsily along the perimeter of the wall. She came to an old badger sett. There was no smell of the animals that occupied it. She enlarged the entrance and made her way inside.

There was protection from rain and also a carpet of dead leaves that had been blown in on the wind together with clumps of sheep's wool. She rested and then time was forgotten as the pains began.

It was her first litter. She longed for Matt, who was always at her side if she felt unwell. She whimpered unhappily, and then was silent. Her cries might bring hunters. She was learning fast.

She needed Matt to soothe her, to take away the pain and the fear. Then the first pup was born. She felt the struggle as he came free. She nosed the tiny bundle, the puppy smell overwhelming her and wakening the knowledge she needed. This was the end product of those weeks when life first began to change for her.

She had no need of teaching. Everything within her told her what to do. She lifted the pup and laid him head down on her crossed paws, right under her nose. She had time before the next one came. She cleared the membrane from his head, licked away the mucus from his mouth, cleaned away the birth coverings and nudged him to feed.

She was aware of purpose. Before she had only known that she had needs, but been unaware of their outcome. Now her protective instinct was roused and nothing and nobody would come between her and her pups.

The seven pups arrived over the next few hours. She was completely absorbed, unaware of noises around her, of the rising wind, or the driving rain that followed. She was safe and she was dry. The pups were sturdy. They pressed against her, each nuzzling a teat. There was milk, almost as soon as the first was born, but she knew that she needed food and water, or her babies would suffer.

She could not get enough of them. She washed them every time they fed, before they slept. She revelled in the feel of the tiny bodies that moved against her, and their soft whimpers. She was aware that these were a danger and she needed to be vigilant.

There were always enemies and though she had no experience, she had the overwhelming mother instinct that would make her fight others to the death to defend her little family.

She left them only briefly during the first twenty four hours, being lucky enough to find a deep puddle where she drank. When the moon crept up the sky on the second night she left them again, needing food. She ached with a ravenous hunger that triggered long suppressed instincts.

Below her on the hill was a tent. Its occupants had driven into town and the site was deserted. There was the scent of humans, but it was old. Nobody was there. She summoned all her courage. The zipped opening frustrated her but she discovered she could crawl underneath the canvas. She crept inside. She found bread and cheese and cooked sausages that had been prepared for the next day's breakfast.

The campers on their return thought a fox had visited them.

The pups were crying for her. There was no sign of trouble on the air and she spread herself so that they could feed. She slept, and woke, absorbed by her new role, and, for the moment, not missing her owners.

Food was a problem. The pups were sturdy and needed all her milk. She did have just enough. Foraging kept her active. She needed long rests to recover from her sorties.

The pups were growing fast and Star was always ravenous.

The changing wind brought an exciting scent of meat and onions cooking. It was familiar and she followed it, hoping it would bring her home. In a caravan at the edge of the woods, a battered and untidy dwelling, lived an elderly couple. Nobody came to that part of the hills and they existed on eggs from a few chickens and on rabbits and hares caught, illegally, in makeshift traps. The chickens were well protected, locked into a henhouse at night. They grew a few vegetables.

Star, following the smell of cooking food, saw the lights of the caravan. She remembered the waste bins in her home, where scavenging was forbidden though at times she was tempted by the wonderful smells of scraps. Some were put in her bowl. Anything unfit for a dog was thrown away, but still enticed her.

There was no bin here as there was no refuse collection. Bottles and tins were buried; food was composted. She discovered there were easy pickings. A battered bucket with a piece of corrugated iron over it held the remains of a chicken, the flesh eaten, the bones used for soup and then discarded. They intended to bury it in the morning. There was little but bones and a few stray scraps of fatty meat. Star knocked off the cover, which fell on soft ground and did not make a noise. The couple slept soundly. They did not hear her. She was as stealthy as any fox, almost completely wild now. There were potato peelings on the compost heap. It and the chicken remains made a small, inadequate meal. Star returned to the pups and fed them, but hunger drove her to hunt again.

She had no success. Her former life had not given her the speed and muscle and cunning she needed to catch her prey. Her clumsiness warned the rabbits and they were safe underground before she could reach them.

There was food of a sort by the caravan, which was only ten minutes away from her den. Star returned for three nights. She found enough to dull the hunger though not to feed her well. On the fourth night a prowling cat, abandoned by its owners and living wild, was there before her. It turned and hissed, then jumped at her. Star moved aside. The cat, determined to keep the food for herself, misjudged her leap, and collided with a tin bucket, which fell off the step on to a small paved area with a mighty crash.

The man woke and swore and threw a boot out of the window. It caught Star on the shoulder. She limped away, hungry, and determined never to go near the caravan again.

21

She hunted in the other direction without success. She needed food. Ranging further she came to a road, where an unwary rabbit had met his death under speeding wheels. She dragged the carcass into the long grass and fed. The body was still warm.

It gave her a new lease of life, and she loped home, free, for the first time since the pups' birth, of hunger pangs.

The road saved her. There was rarely a day without a kill. She was wary of the cars, waiting until the road was empty before she went out to take her finds. Her frequent hunting had improved her speed. Rabbits and pheasants provided her with bounty.

The pups grew. Star learned. Her need taught her. She fared well with mice and young rabbits, and the pups prospered. Soon they were big enough to wander, and curiosity about their world drove them to explore.

Star learned to be as wary as any wild animal. As soon as she heard or saw figures in the distance or smelled humans on the wind, she shepherded the pups into safety, making sure they were well hidden. She guarded the entrance to the den, ready to attack anyone who came near her little family.

Sheep did not forage here, so no farmer was aware of her presence. She hunted at night, when small beasts also came out to play and when the roads were quieter.

The pups learned about wind and wild weather and one night they cowered against Star while thunder rolled, and lightning split the sky. Then came nights of severe frost. There was nothing on the hills for her to hunt. Every creature seemed to have hidden in shelter. One by one the pups began to die. Star grieved for them. Hunger dominated her and the two survivors.

They were foraging with her. Weaning had begun. They were eating grass and the droppings of deer when the blizzard overtook them. Accustomed to milder winters in her home to the south, Star had never seen snow. They sheltered for a while and then went on again, driven by hunger. They found nothing and had to rest. Star found a hollow, out of the wind, but the snow drifted and buried them and she could not dig her way out.

She and the pups discovered that if they licked their cold

covering it melted into water and they could drink. That would keep them alive, but they were so hungry.

They were all at risk.

Star had no choice. They were trapped in her hiding place, which had become a prison. She slept, trying to cuddle them close to keep them warm.

Lying there under the snow, in an uneasy sleep, she dreamed of her own mother and her brothers and sisters. She dreamed of the box they slept in, cuddled up together on a fleecy rug, heat pouring down on them from an overhead lamp. She did not know what it was but she had loved its comfort.

She woke to desolation and tried to cuddle warmth into her body, tried to keep her pups safe. She longed for her lost home. When the pups were old enough she would find her way back. Overcome by misery, forgetting caution, she wailed, a long keening cry that echoed eerily on the hills.

Time passed. The pups whimpered, trying to extract milk that was no longer there. Star was dominated by raging hunger, but she was exhausted, and barely able to think about her pups. There were only the memories that returned in more frequent dreams. Memories of food and warmth and shelter, of people who played with her and took her for walks. Memories of sandy beaches and swimming in the sea. Memories of people who had loved her.

Memories of the day that marked the start of her earlier life. She was nearly seven weeks old and people came daily to look at her and her litter mates, to play with them, and cuddle them. None of them seemed better than any other. Her brothers and sisters found owners, but she stayed unclaimed.

Then Matt came, his wife with him. He had a wonderful voice and hands that stroked her gently. Every fibre of her small body yearned to belong to this man. She fell in love with him when he lifted her and held her close against him, smiling down at her. She was not yet old enough to leave the nest. He came daily. She watched for his visits, for his shape at the door, for his hands reaching down to pet her.

When he went out of the kennel area she waited for his return. He visited several times, and she became more devoted to him. He was fun. He belonged to her and she to him. This was why she had been born. She had no regrets when she was taken from her mother. She loved her new home and its owners more than anything else in life.

Now she was trapped but she longed for Liz and Matt and was still sure Matt would come for her. He always came when she needed him. She waited through the long hours. Her two pups were cold. They burrowed underneath her and she did her best to comfort them and warm them. They needed food but she could not force her way out of their prison.

She ached for that much-loved voice. She had never given up the hope that he would find her. She cocked her head, ears pricked, listening. He had never let her down.

There was only the faint murmur of the wind beyond the drift, and darkness from the covering snow. The pups whimpered. The long hours passed. The snow trap deepened.

Nobody came.

Five

There had been a bad weather warning forecast before they went to bed, but no one had suggested that it would be anything like this.

Greg could not believe the sight that met his eyes when he got up in the morning. Snow lay deep, covering fields and barns and trees, turning the roofs of bungalow and farmhouse to an unfamiliar pristine white. Sun dazzled. There would be no school for Dannie. No visitors to the farm. They were cut off.

He had to find his sheep. There would be too many losses if he left them on the hills. Most of the lambs were as yet young and would be punished by such savage weather. He spent a weary morning fighting his way upwards, Meg floundering beside him.

He needed Rab but the dog's cut paw had become infected and he was too lame to walk far. He cursed the boys who had occupied a dull Sunday afternoon by bringing a load of bottles on to the hill and smashing them with stones. Greg and Sheina had spent over an hour hunting down every tiny bit of splintered glass. He wished he knew who they were. They had run off when he saw them. Rab, chasing after them to warn them off, had cut his paw.

In spite of a very short break for lunch, it was almost teatime before he found the last of his stragglers. To his annoyance, his collie had vanished. He called her, his voice echoing over the silent hills.

'Meg! Meg! Come. Come.'

He might as well have been shouting to a piece of rock. The little bitch had worked hard all afternoon, and now, when they should have been making their way down the hill, she had her nose to the ground and was following some scent of her own.

He should never have brought her out. She was too old, but the sheep were in danger and he had no choice. A rare irritation mastered him. His feet and hands and nose and ears were freezing and he longed for home. As yet they had over half a mile to travel, dusk was falling, and he was herding eighty sheep and their lambs to safety with an ageing dog. Life threw enough problems at him without an unseasonable snowfall at the end of April.

No use being angry with Meg. Under normal circumstances he would never have dreamed of bringing her out on the hill. She was battling arthritis and days like this made it worse. As it did for him. Maybe it was ageing her fast and she was forgetting her training. Where on earth was she?

He continued worrying, sure they were lost. And worst of all, that Meg was also lost. He did not want her out on the hills on a bitter night, and was not sure she could find her way home. All landmarks had vanished. The snow, criss-crossed by the tracks of many birds and animals, covered everything.

Suddenly Meg appeared, coming towards him as fast as she was able. She barked at him, and turned to go up the hill again, as if asking him to follow. Maybe there were more sheep up there. If so, they weren't his, but he would not leave a neighbour's sheep in trouble. They must have strayed or been let out by a careless walker. There was nothing much to be seen, but Meg was making for a hummock on the ground, and once she reached it, she began to dig, her paws frantic.

The snow was several inches deep and made walking diffi-cult. He needed to get home before dark. He needed the sheep down by the house. The forecasters spoke of blizzards during the night. He did not need a daft dog looking for badgers.

There was an odd noise. Certainly not a badger noise.

He walked over and looked down. Meg stopped digging, bent her head down and then lifted it to look at the farmer, her eyes sparkling, a tiny pup in her mouth. She held it up to him. The mite was freezing cold. It was too exhausted to protest when he lifted it.

A little dog, male, surely not more than six weeks old.

26

Maybe older if he had been living wild relying on his mother for food. Brown eyes, filled with fear, looked up at him. This pup knew nothing about humans. He was too weak to do more than growl softly. He did not try to bite. He needed food and care and warmth. Pity for the shivering scrap took over. He couldn't leave him here to die.

The pup struggled feebly, growling softly as Greg lifted him, afraid of this creature that towered above him.

'Calm down, baby,' Greg said softly. 'I'm here to help. I won't hurt you.'

Unable to think of anything else to do with him for the moment, Greg tucked him into his deep pocket where at least it would have warmth. The darkness and security calmed the little creature and he lay still, taking heat from the man who had found him.

Greg was aware of sounds coming from the hummock. Another pup was whimpering. He knelt and dug down. This had once been a badger's sett, long deserted. It was years since he had known of any badgers on the hill.

He stared at the bitch lying just inside the entrance. There was a second pup beside her, a female, her hunger cries feebler than her brother's.

The mother lifted her head and whimpered softly. She was cold and she was exhausted. Greg bent to stroke and reassure her, guessing at her fear. She drew her lips back from her teeth, her eyes filled with terror. Star had almost forgotten kindness from humans. She needed to defend her pups, but a strange familiar feeling overtook her. This man, like Matt, smelled of sheep.

'Sssss,' he said softly. It was the sound that Matt made if she were afraid. 'Sssss. I won't hurt you or your babies. You need help, little girl. Let's have a look at you. Poor little lass. You're so cold.'

His voice, like Matt's, was soft and soothing and his hands were gentle.

Greg felt a sudden flood of anger. What kind of person had let this little bitch loose on the hill with pups? She was almost dead with cold, she was starvation thin, but she was a beautiful dog, come from heaven knew where. He had not heard any mention of a lost bitch, and news travelled fast in

27

these wild lands, high in the Scottish mountains, where neighbour looked out for neighbour and all were ready to help in a crisis.

'I won't hurt you, lass,' he said softly. She gazed up at him.

His hands were as gentle as Matt's had been and he had the same reassuring smell, of sheep and shaving lotion and soap. He was close to Matt's age, too, old enough to be calm and soft-spoken. She was too exhausted to fight him. She looked up at him, her eyes dark with anxiety. Would he help her? Would he take her out of this bleak place? She was so cold that she was almost beyond hunger.

He knelt beside her. He stroked her throat, murmuring all the time, hoping his tone would reassure her. How long had she been out here? The pups must be at least five weeks old. He found one more, lying at the far end of the sett. It had died of cold, probably a day or so before.

Greg had the remains of his lunch in his other pocket. That needed to be emptied for the second pup. He took the last sandwich out of the paper, and dropped it beside the bitch. She pushed it towards the puppy lying beside her, who took it and chewed a little but was too exhausted to do more.

Star ate. The soft voice coaxing her reminded her of days when there had been kind people around her. She thrust her nose into Greg's hand.

'Good girl. Eat it all, then. What are we going to do with you? You don't look up to walking in this. We need to get you home and warm.' The tone and the words soothed her, triggering gentler memories. Greg reached towards her, and gave her a digestive biscuit that he had saved from his tea. Star took it, ate it, and then licked his hand. Her tail wagged feebly. She was so dirty that it was difficult to tell her coat colour but from the shape of her head he thought she was probably a Golden Retriever. She might be cross bred, but he doubted that.

She had lost much of her fur after having the pups and her coat was thin, ending in a scruffy-looking rat tail. That would not help her in this bitter weather. Whatever she was, she was in trouble.

Meg was waiting for his approval.

'Clever Meg,' he said, knowing her need. She wagged her tail furiously, sure she had done well in finding these outcasts. They added to his immediate problems but there was no way he could leave them. He was not sure they would survive even in the time it took to go back to his own farm.

The bitch would be a tidy burden, as she was too weak to walk. But he was used to walking miles carrying lambs. He hoped she would not struggle, or worse, bite in fear.

He tucked the second pup into his other pocket. They would be happier together but there was no room. He lifted the mother, and tucked her inside his coat, hoping that his body would warm her.

Star had lost all her energy. She knew she needed help. She snuggled against him. Greg wondered who had abandoned her. He was used to dogs being dumped because they became too inconvenient or too expensive. Someone elderly who hadn't been able to cope with puppies? Someone who didn't care and didn't want the litter? A couple divorcing and no time for the dog?

He would like to meet them and tell them what he thought of anyone capable of turning out a bitch with pups. She must have been dumped. He knew all the neighbours and not one of them had a dog like this. Or had some caravanner on holiday lost her? But surely they would hunt until they found her?

He had to hurry, and that was not easy in this amount of snow. The sheep needed to be herded to safety in the home field below them. Progress was slow. The bitch was heavy and Greg was afraid of slipping. He would be in dire trouble then, as his wife could not cope with everything if he were unable to walk. He only hoped she had not needed his help tonight. He should have been home hours ago.

Hopefully Dannie would have been enthralled by the snow, and been outside making a snowman. Or would he? The child was so unpredictable. He had been asleep when Greg left just after five that morning.

Star looked up at her rescuer. Her brown eyes spoke to him, though he could not read their message.

'Soon be home and get you warm and fed,' he said, knowing that the sound of his voice would help her relax.

Her tail made a faint movement as if trying to thank him and acknowledge his care. Harsh-voiced strangers were terrifying still, but people like Greg meant warmth and food, she was sure.

The two tiny pups were small weights in his pockets. They nestled quietly, warm for maybe the first time in their short lives. It must have been cold on the hill and their mother was so thin that she must have had little heat in her own body.

It seemed a long half hour before he looked down with thankfulness at the nearby lights that spilled a patchwork of shadows on the yard. He sighed, longing to rest. But there was more work to do. He would take the refugees into the kitchen and then have to bring out swedes for the sheep.

He hoped no lambs would be born in the night. He needed sleep.

It looked as if he had just acquired three more dogs, at least temporarily. He might be able to find them all homes, but not in this condition. It would take time and dedication to restore these waifs to first-class health.

There might have been other pups, besides the dead one he had left on the hill. When the snow had gone he would go back and bury it. He hated to think of predators taking it. He wondered if there had been others, fallen victim to prowling fox or stoat or weasel.

Darkness was only a heartbeat away and it was beginning to freeze. He whistled to Meg and made his way carefully downwards.

The wind whipped icy flakes into his face. Meg shook herself. The snow was so deep that she floundered, but she struggled on. Her place was beside her master. Her thoughts were on food and the rug by the Aga where she was allowed to lie on these bitter nights.

At last they were home. He laid Star in the snow and opened the gate for Meg to drive the sheep into safety and then smiled with enormous relief when he saw the piles of swedes. His flock rushed to feed. He closed the gate, and picked up the bitch again. The pups were stirring in his pockets. He hoped they could breathe.

There would be little rest. His new acquisitions needed

food. They needed a vet, too, but there was no way that his local vets and friends, Angus and his son Jamie, could reach them tonight.

The shine from the kitchen window added an inviting patchwork glow to that of the security lights that were always on after dark. There was a large oddly-shaped snowman just beyond the kitchen door, the ground around it well marked with small footprints and some of Sheina's. It wore one of Greg's old hats, set at a rakish angle. Its coal eyes glittered, the carrot nose stuck out at an odd angle and the mouth had been made from a red pepper. The farmer smiled at the lopsided creation. So Dannie had been busy. Maybe he would be tired after some time in the cold air and hard work.

He hoped the child had gone to bed. He was too old to cope with a six-year-old, especially one with Dannie's problems. Had Shelley been such a handful when she was the same age? It was so long ago. He couldn't remember. Memory brought back only a laughing little girl, eager to ride her pony or feed the latest orphan lambs.

Dannie was so different. He had lived on the farm for a year but he avoided the sheep and the poultry whenever possible. He wouldn't go near the pigs. He said they smelled. He had tried to tease the dogs, but both Meg and Rab had warned him off with a growl and a lifted lip and he no longer took liberties with them.

They seemed to have a pact. You leave us alone and we won't hurt you. The dogs ignored the child, and he ignored them. They had greeted Shelley rapturously, though. Meg remembered her from their short visits, but Rab had never met her before. They were now used to the wheelchair. It was part of Shelley.

Greg wondered if Shelley herself would ever be used to it. There was too much time to think alone in the hills and somehow his thoughts these days seemed to centre round his daughter and her son. One moment in time . . . and so many lives were altered for ever.

Six

Greg opened the inner door and stepped into the kitchen, ducking his head in the doorway. As always, he felt as if he had come into a haven of warmth and light. The heat hit him.

His wife, busy laying the table for his meal, turned to smile at him.

It was hard to return her smile. His cheeks seemed to have become numb. His face ached, and his ears felt as if they were lumps of frost. His hands began to tingle.

'Best present I could have had,' he said.

'Present?' Sheina looked bewildered.

'The swedes you put out for the sheep. Thank you. I was dreading going out again.'

'Dannie helped me. He's been very good for a change. He's been so busy he actually wanted to go to bed and he's sound asleep. Shelley's in her room, watching her favourite soap. You're very late.'

Greg was thankful that his daughter and her son had separate quarters in the house. He needed rest and peace. A lively six-year-old, racing around, allowed little of that when he was with them.

Greg glanced at his watch. Seven o'clock. The detour to find the bitch and her pups had taken more time than he realized.

His hands and feet and ears were returning painfully to warmth. Meg was shivering too in spite of her thick coat. So was the bitch who lay against him under his jacket. Only the occasional shaking and the faint rise and fall of her chest as she breathed showed him she had not yet given up.

He laid her on the rug in front of the big Aga. He brushed the snow from Meg's black and white fur with the towel that hung there, ready to dry the dogs. Her grey muzzle reproached him. Meg was so willing. She loved coming with him, even though it tired her.

He patted her head. 'You're a faithful old thing, aren't you?' he said, and, in spite of her weariness, the collie wagged an enthusiastic tail.

Sheina looked down at the newcomer and raised her eyebrows even higher when Greg took the two pups from his pocket.

'Meg found her on the hill,' Greg held them out to his wife. They smelled, and were in dire need of a bath.

'Where on earth did they come from?'

'Goodness knows. I'd guess she's been living there some time judging by the state she's in, and trying to feed the pups for herself. Bert and Mary in the caravan said they thought there was a stray dog living near them, but they never saw her. Only heard her and the pups. They think she was raiding their bin, but it could have been a stray cat that's also been hanging around.'

Sheina knelt beside Star and put the pups against her. They sought in vain for the milk that had now dried up. There were bottles for the lambs, ready to use. Sheina looked down at the little mother.

'This one is going to take some saving,' she said. 'I wonder how she got there? She must have had the pups in the wild. Someone's been either very cruel or very careless.'

She brought a thick rug and put it over the refugee. Slowly Star relaxed as warmth penetrated her chilled body. With warmth came returning strength. She did not resist when Sheina brought her special cure, the little phial of Rescue Remedy that always stood on the dresser, ready for use in any emergency. Corpse reviver, their vet Jamie called it, and it certainly was that. She had brought back to life a litter of kittens that had been born in the barn to a stray cat that had died before they were a day old. Meg found them and alerted her. Sheina always kept a stock of the remedies in the drawer that was filled with remedies for sick animals. Star savoured the taste. She did not protest when Sheina lifted each pup to give it its dose. They too liked this new flavour.

Star began to look about her, to sniff the air, asking what

was there. The house was reviving memories. There were familiar smells of washing-up liquid and floor polish; of cooking food, which made her salivate. A small radio, tuned to Classic FM, was playing soothing music.

She had known places like this before. The only thing strange to her was the big grandfather clock in the corner that suddenly chimed the hour. She listened, her head on one side, and then relaxed. It was just furniture, and that did not move about. Rab came to sniff her. He nosed her and then lay beside her. Meg came to the other side and cuddled against her as if aware this newcomer needed warmth and reassurance.

Star lay, savouring the warmth and the presence of kind people. No need to go hunting. No need for fear. She could rest.

Greg dropped into the big shabby armchair. Although he was so tired, he looked around him with contentment. They were safe. He loved his home.

'Orphans of the storm. They need a lot of TLC,' his wife said, looking down at the little family.

Greg grabbed her wrist. 'So do I,' he said, suddenly realizing that for some time on the hill he had been afraid he would fall and be unable to get up and would die out there in the snow. He pulled her to him and kissed her. His lips were ice cold.

'Brrrr. You're frozen. That was like being kissed by a ghost,' his wife said, laughing. Greg was rarely demonstrative. His homecoming was reassurance to both of them after a dreadful day. 'Get warm, for goodness sake.'

This was his favourite room, always embracing him with its familiarity. It was very large and, though modernized, there was still room for the old table that his grandmother used to scrub, and for the big armchairs, needing new covers and stuffing, that offered far more comfort than any modern suite. Greg refused to part with them. They were home. Sheina's collection of model animals covered every vacant space.

'You've got two hundred and ninety-three dogs and cats and horses and owls, and elephants,' Dannie said on one of his better afternoons, having been inspired to go through the house and count them. 'I'll buy you a giraffe. Then you'll have two hundred and ninety-four.'

Sheina laughed, entertained by the thought of a giraffe's long neck standing out among the dogs and cats.

There were china figurines, bronze models and a few old ivories left to her by her father, ranged on every sill and mantelshelf. The problem was that those who saw them always knew what to give them for Christmas or birthday. Another model.

'We'll have to build a special house for them,' Sheina had said, laughing, as she added six more to her collection last Christmas. Greg enjoyed them. Many had memories. One large china collie, in their bedroom, was a souvenir of Shelley's first sheepdog trial, although she hadn't won. Shelley didn't want it where she could see it. It was too poignant a reminder of the days when she could walk and run and live the same kind of life as everybody else.

The big kitchen looked different tonight. It took a moment for him to realize that it was brightened by vividly embroidered cushions in the big arm chairs and a new, elaborately patterned multi-coloured rug.

Greg raised his eyebrows, and looked at his wife.

'Been spending our hard-earned cash?'

Sheina smiled, her face suddenly losing several years.

'No. They're presents from Shelley. She's been working on them for weeks, as a thank-you for looking after Dannie while she was in hospital. She started them while she was in the hospital. Occupational therapy. It's another thing she can still do. She's had a good day today. No physiotherapist to make her try to move.'

Greg looked at the cushions and admired the intricate design and unusual colouring of the rug.

'She's clever,' he said. 'Wonder where she gets it from? Not from me, that's for sure. Maybe she could make them to sell . . . she needs an occupation. It might not be so different from the job she had in London.'

Rab, having satisfied his curiosity about the newcomer, wanted attention. He walked over to Greg and sat beside him, nose on his knee, his brown eyes reproachful. His paw hurt and he had been left behind, unbelievably, when Greg went out that morning. They never went out without him.

The dog had sat on the windowsill watching them go, his forlorn howls following his master up the hill. It taken nearly an hour for Sheina to comfort him. The snowman helped all of them. Rab limped happily around as they built it. Sheina had covered the bandaged paw with a homemade polythene boot to keep him dry. He was overjoyed to be useful and carried the hat and various other bits which he found and offered. His antics made Dannie laugh, which was a rare event.

Sheina was glad that she had brought the dog out. She tried to leave him indoors, but he scratched at the door and wailed until she decided to let him join them. Even so, she kept a careful eye on him. They needed him.

The deep cut on Rab's front pad was a small disaster. Luckily when it first happened the vet was due to look at their Jersey cow, who was off her feed. She was a descendent of one of Greg's sillier investments, he thought, thanks to a six-year-old daughter longing for one of the caramel-coloured beauties for her own. Jerseys were delicate animals and needed extra care in these bleak Highlands.

Toffee was eight years old now, and had had health problems much of her life, but she was part of the family and nobody would dream of parting with her. They had no milking herd and Toffee provided their household needs. There was always a waiting list for her calves. Her milk gave them cream and when Sheina was not too busy she made butter and cottage cheese. She had no time for the cheeses for which she had once been famous.

Toffee often spent warm days looking in through the kitchen window as if wondering what Sheina did in there. She wandered freely round the yard and inspected the wheelchair in great detail, ending with washing Shelley's face with her tongue, which did make their daughter laugh. Toffee adored people.

'I think she thinks she's a dog, really,' Shelley said. 'There's nothing like sitting in the sun with a cow for company.'

Shelley was little older than her own small son when Greg bought Toffee's great grandmother. Where had all that time gone?

'Vet been?' he asked as he stroked Rab, who was in danger of hurting his injured paw as he danced around his master in frantic greeting. Sheina was better at bandaging than any of the professionals.

Sheina was busy at the Aga.

'Angus came before the snow set in. He was worried about Toffee. As well as the mastitis he had to let gas out of her after you'd gone. He thinks she'll be OK now. And Jamie promised he'd be over as soon as the weather improves.'

'It'll be good to see him again. Angus must be pleased that he decided to come home and work in partnership. Maybe he can cheer Shelley up. They were good friends at school.'

She turned to him, holding the big ladle she was using to stir the pot that always sat there, ready to provide instant warmth for anyone who had been out in the cold.

'That was a long time ago. Angus had a look at the black ewe. Says there'll be twins in the morning and there shouldn't be a problem. She's safe in the barn.'

Star gulped down a very small bowl of stew. Sheina was afraid of overfeeding an animal that might be near to starvation. Within minutes of eating the Retriever was asleep, revelling in warmth and comfort.

Sheina picked up one of the pups.

'I wouldn't think ewes' milk would harm them?' she said, more of a question than a statement.

'Might upset tummies for a day or two, but they look old enough to wean,' Greg said.

She offered the dog pup a bottle, but he had no idea how to suck. He tried to bite her, afraid of the touch of human hands. She took a little meat from the meal that was waiting, then blew on it to cool it and fed it to the puppy, holding it on her finger so that when he licked at it he would learn her smell and associate her with food and not fear.

Greg fed the second. 'Little and often,' he said. 'Too much could kill them.'

Sheina wrinkled her nose.

'I don't need teaching to suck eggs. First job is to bathe them. They smell disgusting. I wonder how long it will take to get them fit and bonny? Nobody would want them in this condition.'

'I wouldn't let anyone have them in this condition,' Greg said. 'Need experts like us on the job.'

The tin bath in the scullery was big enough for both the pups. Neither liked the soapy water or the hard rubbing that was needed to get their matted fur clean, but the warmth helped restore their strength.

Sheina's pup was covered in dried-on mud and she had a worse job than Greg. By the time she had picked up a rough towel to rub her mite dry, Greg had finished his chore and the little dog pup was lying on a thick spread of newspaper by the Aga. He made no attempt to move, but lay watching, baffled by the many new smells and sensations and the strange objects that surrounded him.

Much of his life up to now had been cold and hunger. At first there had been warmth from his mother and the other pups, but gradually that warmth vanished. As did the other pups, falling victim to the cold. He and his sister were often alone while their mother hunted, desperate to find enough food to keep them from starvation. They crept together in a small huddle for comfort.

Greg looked down on him, and stroked the small head with a finger. The pup stared up anxiously, hoping that this huge creature meant no harm and would continue to bring him warmth and food. He was a chunky little animal, and had obviously been fed fairly well during his time on the hill. His mother had done her very best for him. His golden fur betrayed his ancestry.

He stood with his tiny paws against the big man's leg. He was still a little nervous of these unfamiliar giants, but he ached for comfort and mothering. Greg picked him up, aware of his need, his huge warm hands enveloping the little body.

'Meg,' he called and put the two pups in her basket. Meg knew her job. She had been surrogate mother for lambs for more than ten years now. She had had three litters of her own and she adored puppies. She curled herself round them and licked the two newcomers. They snuggled against her, and slept. Sheina piled thick layers of newspaper round the bed and enclosed it in the portable puppy pen. That at least would isolate the mess when they began to rouse. Greg was sponging Star, cleaning her fur. Star lay still, delighted to be groomed again. That had been a favourite part of her day.

'Angus left a course of antibiotics for Rab. There's enough for ten days.'

She went over to the Aga again to dish out the stew.

'We need him to look at them as soon as this lot clears,' she said. 'I hope it doesn't last three weeks like it did two years ago.'

Star curled up on the rug again, nose on paws, and watched as Greg and Sheina ate.

'Can't wait for bed,' Greg said.

It was only nine o'clock but he would go up to bed early, and hopefully have a few hours' sleep before the black ewe lambed. He ached all over after battling with the cold and the snow.

He stretched out his legs, watching Star as Timbo, their big tabby, came into the room. Star was used to cats. She opened one eye but had no energy. She went to sleep again. The cat stared at her, decided she was no threat and jumped to the window sill where he sat looking out at the snowy yard, which glittered in the shine of the security lights.

Greg looked down at his new protégé.

'I wonder what her name is? We have to call her something and I doubt if we can pick on anything she'll recognize.'

The door was opened so suddenly that it banged against the wall as Shelley wheeled herself in. The dog jumped and then settled, though Star kept a wary eye on this unexpected newcomer. She had seen wheelchairs before when out with her former master.

'Dad.' Shelley spoke so fast he could not distinguish the words.

She sounded frantic.

Her voice was choked.

'Slow down, love. What's wrong?'

Shelley took a deep breath before she spoke again.

'I went into Dannie's room when my programme ended to say good night and tell him a story if he was still awake. His bed was empty, the window was open and the room's freezing. He's dressed himself and gone out into the snow. His wellies and anorak and hat are missing. I looked round the other rooms, thinking he might be in the bathroom, but there isn't a sign of him.'

'I'll look for him. He can't be far. He probably wanted to make another snowman.'

Sheina was in the annexe, bottle feeding the first of three orphan lambs. She looked up as Greg came into the room and frowned.

'He's always threatening to run away, to go back to where they lived before. But to take off tonight, in this . . . surely he wouldn't.'

'He's too young to understand the danger. I hope he's not gone far,' Greg said, worry needling him. As if they hadn't enough bother without this. 'Otherwise, he hasn't a chance. Come on, Meg. You're all I've got. We must find Dannie.'

He moved the pen to let the collie out, and then put it back again round the two pups. They might explore and harm themselves once they recovered their strength. The door slammed as he went out into the yard.

Shelley, worry flooding her, followed her mother into the annexe. She needed occupation. Her thoughts raced round her head, one disaster scenario following another. She could at least bottle feed a lamb. The little beast was hungry and sucked lustily, occupying only part of Shelley's thoughts. Where was Dannie? Why had he gone? If he was out too long in the snow . . . if only she had the use of her legs and could help her father hunt for him.

Fear whirled round her head. The same devastating thought came back to plague her. Why did I let David drive that night?

If only she could roll time back. No use thinking about that. The teat almost came off the bottle and she concentrated on the task in hand. The lamb was well grown and lusty, sucking with all his strength. His warm body was a comfort, taking her back to childhood days when this had been her favourite chore.

Rab was also in the annexe. The door was shut. Star woke. She could not join her pups, safely enclosed inside the wire pen. It was dangerous to be alone. Bad things happened when people went away leaving empty rooms. She crawled out from under the rug that Sheina had put over her. She needed her pups. They had to be protected. They were locked away from her, inside the wire pen that Sheina had put to keep them safe.

Outside Greg hunted in vain. There wasn't a sign of his grandson. The snow had covered his tracks. It was beginning to fall again, great soft white flakes that clung to eyebrows and nose and covered Meg's black and white fur.

'Dannie,' he called. 'Dannie!'

His voice echoed, mocking him, but there was no reply.

Seven

Greg had to find Dannie. He did not know where to look. The darkness beyond the reach of the security lights was absolute. There were so many outbuildings on the farm.

There were distant lights on the faraway hills, telling of neighbours who under other circumstances would come and help search, but they were cut off.

Snow drifted against the doors of the barns and pigsties, against the farm door itself, blown by an irritable wind that carried hints of the Arctic in its teeth.

'Dannie! Dannie!'

The shouts triggered fear in Star. In the annexe Shelley reached for a glass of water and knocked it to the floor. The crash echoed. There had been the sound of breaking glass before when Star had been alone. She had been left behind one evening while her owners went off in their car.

That night there was smashed glass, followed by thumping feet and men's voices and meat had been thrown to her. A luscious lump of raw steak, a treat never seen before. She wolfed it. Then the world began to spin and rough hands seized her and carried her. She knew no more for some time but when she woke she was lying in the back of a jolting van on dirty straw.

Greg's shouts reminded her of the men. The sound of broken glass triggered terror. She was alone. Meg was with her master, and Rab was in the annexe. This time she was wary. Nobody but Star could protect her pups. She tried to push the pen away from them, but it would not move. They woke and came to the wire, trying in their turn to reach her, whimpering for her. She jumped on to the armchair beside the pen and then jumped over and curled herself round her babies. No one would take her. She would defend them with her life.

Greg continued to call. Surely Dannie couldn't have gone far. Surely he must hear his grandfather's voice? Or was he lying somewhere with a broken leg, or unconscious in deep snow, perhaps even in a drift, hypothermia waiting to claim him?

Anger flared, drowning worry. If David hadn't driven that night, none of this would have happened. He wished the clock back with a passion that shook him. No use crying over what was past. He called to Meg.

'Find him, lass. There's a good lass. Find Dannie. Dannie!'

He shouted again and inside the farmhouse Star trembled with fear. The men had shouted. Any moment now they would invade her peace and she and the pups would be taken back to the misery on the hills and the cold and the hunger.

'Dannie!'

The cold was numbing. Where was he?

Meg tracked through the unbroken snow, but found no trace of his scent. The small boy had vanished completely. Greg looked at the barns again. Dannie was afraid of the biggest barn. One of the casual hands they had employed told the child that there had been a murder there. A man had killed one of the milkmaids and then hanged himself. It wasn't even true. Dannie had nightmares for weeks. The man was sacked.

Why had Dannie run away and why tonight of all nights? It was bitterly cold and freezing hard. Greg beat his hands against his sides. He had forgotten his gloves. His fingers were almost numb. Dannie would not have thought of gloves. Suppose he had climbed the big five-barred gate? It was too heavy for him to open but he loved clambering over it. They always stopped him because it led to the little lane and then the busy road.

The child had been growing more disturbed over the last weeks. They all felt helpless, unable to find out what he was thinking.

Greg spent much of his time worrying, desperately trying to think of a way of helping Dannie. He was an urban child, used to a big town and all its facilities. He didn't like the mountains. He wanted busy streets and people all round him; he wanted the adventure playground in the park. He wanted

43

fish and chips and pizzas, not the nourishing meals that Sheina always made.

He wanted his old school, his old friends, his familiar routine. And above all, he wanted his father. Here, more than four hundred miles away from the place where he had been born, the child felt alien, and Greg knew it. What he did not know was how to counteract those feelings.

Shelley had her own unhappiness and difficulties. The year she had spent in hospital had not helped at all. Dannie knew David's parents well, as they lived near his old home, and visited often. They also visited Shelley. Greg and Sheina envied them. Hospital visits were impossible for them. The farm and the needs of the animals tied them as surely as if they were chained.

Life had been easier once. There were always people free to help in times of need on any farm in the area. Now everyone was struggling against ever-rising costs. The Foot and Mouth epidemic of 2001 had hit the whole country with devastating effect, and though Greg and Sheina had, mercifully, been spared its ravages, the farming industry as a whole had suffered such a blow that nobody had spare time to help out. A visit to the special unit in the South where Shelley was taken when her back injuries were diagnosed meant at least two days away if not more.

Sheina wrote daily. They sent cards, they sent flowers, they sent little gifts. They phoned. They occupied themselves with the alterations to the farmhouse. She would never walk again, the doctors said. They could only agonize.

Dannie didn't really know them before the accident. They only saw the child for a brief long weekend once a year, when Shelley and David made flying visits. Had Dannie decided to try and reach his other grandparents? They had been frequent visitors, living only twenty miles from their son's home.

Dannie had a host of toys. Grandpa John gave me this. Grandma Lois gave me that. Grandpa John took me to the circus. Can we go to the circus? They sent presents to the child still, and Grandma Lois sent him a postcard every week, with pictures of places they had visited together. Greg thought it a bad idea, but how could he write or phone and say so?

They were also the child's grandparents and had had far more to do with him than Greg and Sheina. If only Shelley had married a local man with local parents. Life was never that simple.

Suppose Dannie had tried to hitchhike? Few people would offer a lift to a child so young, but there was always the odd one, and there danger lay. Suppose he had been abducted? But the snow must have prevented vehicles coming down the lane.

He thought back to those early days, when they had tried so hard to help the child and hoped he would learn to love them. Dannie had gone home with his babysitter after the police had told her of the accident. He had been bewildered and silent when Sheina came two days later to take him to their home. He had been such a quiet child. He was just five years old then. How much did he understand of what had happened?

One of the few people who did manage to get through to him was the vet. Angus had no grandchildren, and always found time to talk to Dannie when he visited the farm. He brought presents; a discarded horse shoe, a glittering pebble that he said contained fool's gold; a slate cat, that he told Dannie was over a million years old – not the cat, but the slate. The child was fascinated.

Angus seemed dismayed when Dannie suddenly confided in him as he was drinking a cup of coffee outside in the yard. Greg was coming out of the barn, after settling a ewe who had just produced triplets after extreme difficulties. It was some months before Shelley came home.

'Gran won't tell me why Mummy has gone away with Daddy. She says Daddy's dead and in Heaven with God, and God wanted him. I hate God. She says Mummy can't walk and the hospital's trying to make her better. I don't believe it. They just don't want me any more.'

'Of course they want you, Dannie,' Angus said. 'I'm afraid it's true, though. Your Mummy was very badly hurt. She will come home, but not yet. The hospital have to help her to get better.'

Angus caught Greg's look and saw that he had heard the exchange. Greg didn't know whether to tell the child he had overheard or to leave it and hope that Dannie would reveal his feelings to them.

'Leave it for now,' Angus said, when the child had gone indoors. 'He's lost trust. Time will help.'

Time seemed to have made very little difference.

Dannie appeared to have almost forgotten his mother when she did come home. It had been impossible to take him to visit her, and the child found phone calls difficult and after a few attempts refused to speak or listen.

When his mother came to the farm Dannie avoided her, and refused to bring her things that she needed. He shouted at her when she couldn't get out of the wheelchair and come to him if he was at the other side of the room.

'You could do it if you tried. You've still got legs. Why don't you try?'

Life handed out some very raw deals.

Greg trudged on, his thoughts bleak. He was so tired. He had to search every inch of the farmyard, and the surroundings. It was a big place. There were so many crannies where a child might hide. The snow had turned to sleet. He pulled his collar up around his face. Meg plodded on, and he felt guilty at bringing her out again, but her sensitive nose might make all the difference, if only she could keep going.

His thoughts became more and more unhappy as he shone the torch into every corner, hunted in doorways and along the fence.

'Dannie. Dannie. Can you hear me? It's Grandad. Call out to me. Where are you?'

Greg racked his brains. The nearest neighbours were over a mile away. He surely wouldn't have tried walking along the road outside the farm? He could never make that distance, as the snow lay deep in the hilly lanes. Suppose he was in a drift?

Suppose someone had seen him and picked him up, with malice in his mind? Few cars ever came along here. It was a dead end. That couldn't have happened. Who on earth would drive along here in this weather? No casual strangers, that was for sure. All the same, the thought returned, and added yet another worry to those he already had.

If they didn't find the child soon . . .

Dannie had a computer. It had been a gift from his father, and he played with it all the time. Suppose he had been talking to someone on the Internet and they had arranged to meet?

Greg had visions of a small dead body being revealed when the snow melted.

They needed a search party fast, but there was no way that anyone could reach them. He had tried to phone his neighbour, to ask if he had seen Dannie, even though he knew it unlikely. But the phone was dead. They were completely isolated.

He trudged on, leaving a dark trail of footsteps behind him. If only Dannie had waited until the snow stopped falling. They could have tracked him then.

Greg went on calling.

'Dannie. Dannie. Dannie.'

There was no answer. Only a teasing echo.

Morning was a long way away and they might be too late.

Eight

Outside the security lights shone on trampled snow. Greg had quartered every corner of the yard. His hopes were fading. He could not think of any place he had not searched except the big barn that Dannie thought was haunted. The child would not go within yards of it. He would never have gone inside, but Greg had to try. There was nowhere else.

Searching the barn would be a problem. It was enormous. Half of it was filled with hay bales, piled high. Dannie could have slipped in among them and be completely hidden. If he was asleep, he would not hear anyone calling. It was also their junkyard for disused machinery, much of which was a trap in itself for a small inquisitive boy. The tractor was kept there too. The barn might not be haunted but there were certainly rats, and Dannie would be terrified of those. He surely wouldn't have gone in there.

As he crossed the yard the lights went out.

He stood, blinded by the sudden darkness. Within minutes there were lights inside the house as Sheina found the emergency lamps. She came out of the house, holding a small torch, which flashed around until she caught Greg in its beam. She also had the big hand-lamp, which she handed to him.

'That's all we need,' she said. 'I was afraid it would happen. I recharged the battery yesterday, thinking you might need it in the fields if we missed a ewe about to give birth. I'll start the generator.'

Some things did go right, Greg thought, impelled to thank God for a supportive and far-thinking wife.

He shone the torch so that Sheina could see her way. They were always prepared for sudden dark as power failures came invariably with snow or high winds. Within minutes the generator was throbbing and the lights were on again, though they flickered. The engine produced a consoling steady thump.

Sheina went back into the kitchen. She had come out of the annexe through another door. She shone her torch towards the pen. Star was with her puppies, her lips drawn back in a snarl.

Sheina spoke, very softly.

'Calm down, little lass. Nothing will hurt you. Calm down now.'

The sudden darkness dismayed Star, and though the lights were reassuring, the steady throb of the generator worried her. She was trembling and her eyes were wild. Her tail was tucked underneath her, firmly clamped as if it would never be lifted to wave again. She growled, now unsure of herself. The feeling of safety had vanished. Strange things happened all the time.

Sheina knelt by the pen, murmuring, until fear died out of the brown eyes.

Shelley came out of the annexe, needing both hands for her wheelchair.

'Thank God for light,' she said. 'Do you remember the prayer for light that you used to read to me?'

'A grace for light. I'd forgotten that,' Sheina said. 'We only had the generator then. Electricity has made such a huge difference, but you end up taking it for granted. How did it go?'

'I only remember bits.' Shelley made coffee for both of them. She needed to be occupied. 'One verse went, "Herself 'ud take the rushlight and light it for us all, And 'God be praised,' she would say – 'now we have a light."''

'It ends "Nor a child in all the nine glens that knows the grace for light." I've still got that book somewhere. Maybe Dannie would be interested.'

If we find him. The same thought crossed both minds. Dannie hated the dark. They had visions of a small terrified boy crouched somewhere out there, away from help, perhaps in a place where they couldn't find him and rescue would be too late. It was a very cold night and it was snowing again. Hypothermia was a killer.

Sheina turned to Star to distract herself. The dog seemed

49

to have reverted to her wild state. Maybe she was upset by the thumping of the generator, which must be something she had never heard before. Sheina did not know that the problem had been caused by the sound of breaking glass.

'It won't hurt you,' Sheina said, seeing the worried look and the anxious set of the long floppy ears. Star was still unsure, but the sounds that had frightened her tonight had not been succeeded by shouting men or thumping feet in heavy boots. The intruders had known the house was empty and isolated so had not bothered to keep quiet.

Outside Greg was beginning to lose hope. Meg was tiring. It was an effort to move one leg in the front of the other. Worry escalated with each passing moment. There was nowhere left now but the big barn. He crossed the yard. What if they didn't find the child? How long could he go on searching? He was so cold and it had been an exhausting day. If he collapsed they would all be in trouble.

No ambulance could reach them. They were marooned without any possibility of medical help until the snow cleared. Dannie might need hospitalization. What then?

How could they face the rest of the evening, and the night? None of them would sleep unless the child was found, and that seemed more and more unlikcly as the minutes passed. How could he return and sit in the warm when he knew the little boy was outside and alone? Why had he gone? And where had he gone?

Greg felt as if the questions would go on and on repeating in his head. He felt so helpless. On any other night he could have rung his neighbours and the police and they would have had a search party. Not just one elderly man and a very old dog.

He ached for Dannie and for Shelley. He knew she wanted to be there with him, to be doing something to find her son. Anger returned. David, David, he thought, if only you knew what you had condemned us all to for the rest of our lives. The anger lent him new vigour. Meg was close to him, looking up at him, as if asking what in the world they were doing out here in the snow. She ought to have been lying by the Aga, recovering her strength for tomorrow. What new disaster would daylight bring?

The snow had stopped and the clouds parted. A half moon shone out of an inky sky, one star alone beside it. Dannie loved the moon, especially the new crescent.

'Wish upon the moon,' he would say.

He always refused to tell his wish because then it would never come true. Greg suspected that it never would come true. He wanted his father.

The doorway of the barn gaped open, inky black inside. There were lights. He hoped they wouldn't overload the generator when he switched them on. The thudding engine resounded in his head. He always forgot how noisy it was. The connection to the main grid had been a major boon. David's huge life insurance had paid for that too. That at least had come quickly. Shelley was still waiting for compensation for the accident. He stood in the barn doorway and listened, but the generator drowned all smaller noises. He went inside.

Sheina stood at the window for a moment, trying to see where Greg had gone.

It was impossible to settle. Impossible to stop the thoughts swirling round her head. She had to be positive for Shelley's sake, but she had almost given up hope.

How long had Dannie been outside? Had he climbed out of the window the moment his mother left him, or had he waited? Shelley, sure he was asleep, had watched television for over two hours. He might now have been missing for over four hours.

Every minute that passed meant Dannie was more at risk. She suddenly hated the farm and its isolation. The parting clouds allowed the moon to shine on unbroken white without a sign of life except for the greyish sheep huddled together in the two fields adjoining the farm.

There was no sign of Greg. She turned back to the room, letting the curtain drop.

Shelley moved her wheelchair from her place beside the Aga to the table. Sheina picked up the two mugs. At least making frequent cups of coffee kept them occupied. Shelley spooned in sugar, scarcely noticing what she was doing.

'Why did he run off?' she asked. 'I'm useless as a mother. I don't know what he's thinking. He won't let me comfort

51

him. He used to cuddle up against me when I read a story. Now he sits like a coiled spring and barely listens. Or he shouts at me to go away, he wants to go to sleep. Mum, what can I do?'

'It's early days,' Sheina said. She reached up to the shelf where the cake tin lived, well out of Dannie's reach, even if he stood on a chair. She took the tin down and looked at the picture. A small boy standing beside three lambs. Dannie would never go near the lambs. She hoped he might want to bottle feed them, but he refused. 'Give him time.'

She cut a thick slab of cake and put it on Shelley's plate. Shelley crumbled it, her thoughts racing. She shivered suddenly.

'It's so cold out there. He must be frightened. He wouldn't have thought about being alone, about the snow cutting us off. He can't have left the farm . . . that road always has thick drifts at the bottom of the hill.'

The road dipped sharply and then rose steeply. Drifts deep enough to bury a child.

Both women hid their thoughts. If Dannie had fallen into it . . .

'I always wished we lived nearer,' Shelley said. 'He was an adorable baby. He was always determined . . . the terrible twos were just that. Raging tantrums if we stopped doing him what he wanted, and he wanted so much.'

She stirred her coffee, and paused to drink.

'He always wanted to run fast, to climb high, to see what was round the next corner. Once he took off on his tricycle and was two miles away before anyone noticed him and realized he was too little to be on his own. The police brought him back. He thought it wonderful to ride in a police car and was cross because they wouldn't sound the sirens. He was only three years old.'

'A little trooper,' the policeman had said. 'This one needs watching.'

He was an inventive child and thought up so much mischief.

Shelley needed to distract herself. She picked up the spoon to stir her coffee but dropped it on the floor. Star, watching anxiously, felt a sudden need to pick it up. It had always been her duty to bring anything that fell on the floor to either Matt or Liz.

The urge was so strong that she whimpered, asking to be noticed, asking to be allowed to do as she had been trained.

Shelley looked at the Retriever and wheeled her chair towards the pen. Star waited expectantly, sure she would be allowed to remove the offending object, but Sheina picked it up and put it in the sink. Star lay down again, her nose on her paws, disconsolate. They hadn't understood.

Shelley was glad of the distraction. She was also glad that the insistent ticking of the grandmother clock was drowned by the noise of the generator. Tick. Tick. Dannie's still in the cold. The minutes were ticking his life away. She looked down at the newcomer. Star's coat, though thin, was matted, especially behind her ears. The fur clumped in huge knots that were going to be painful when combed.

'She's a mess, but she has a pretty face. When she's put on some weight and got her coat back she'll look lovely. Are you going to keep her?' Shelley asked.

'Too soon to say. Someone might be looking for her and if so we can send her to her real owners. I'd guess from the way she behaves with us that she has had a good home.'

'Something spooked her tonight when she was left alone. I wonder what has happened to her in recent weeks? Those pups must have been born on the hill.'

Sheina made another cup of coffee. They didn't need it but it filled in the time. Greg must be freezing. She wondered whether to take him across a mug, but decided against it. He'd only refuse it, anxious to keep searching. Surely he would find Dannie soon?

They drank in silence. Shelley picked up the knife and cut another slice of cake for each of them. She had always loved cooking. It was something she could still do. It was years since Sheina and Greg had been so well supplied with pies and tarts and scones and various kinds of cake.

'One of Gran's cut and come again recipes,' she said. 'At least I can still cook. Some people starve when they're worried sick. I pig it.'

You always did, Sheina thought, remembering a small girl

racing in from school, shouting breathlessly:'I've had an awful day. Where's the cake?'

Yet she never put on weight. Unlike me, her mother thought. Cake was the last thing she ought to be eating.

'It's every bit as good as Gran's,' Sheina said, after two mouthfuls.

'There are things I can still do, like feed us,' Shelley said. 'It's so stupid, being stuck in one place unable to move. Why won't my wretched legs obey me?'

It was a frequent topic, especially after the physiotherapist had called.

Sheina rallied her thoughts, which were outside with Greg and were filled with fear for Dannie.

'There's lots you can still do. Look at the wheelchair Olympics and that TV presenter. She goes all over the place in her chair and you completely forget she can't walk. America had a President in a wheelchair.'

'I wish Dannie would accept it,' Shelley said. 'He's convinced I have some deep dark secret reason for not trying . . . just to make him have to do things he doesn't want to do, like tidying his room or clearing away his dishes from the table.'

She cut another slice of cake.

'I ought not to be able to eat,' she said. 'I feel if I do it will take away the emptiness. I want, so much, to walk again. I try . . . I can stand for a second but then my legs give way. I keep thinking . . .'

Her voice tailed away, unwilling to express her feelings.

They sat in silence, neither wishing to voice the thoughts that now dominated them. Thoughts of a small boy, plodding alone through the snow, getting colder and colder, maybe falling down. And then . . .

Star watched them, aware of the odd atmosphere in the room. Shelley, turning her chair suddenly, knocked over a small table on which were two pens and the remote control for the television set. Irritated, she shouted her annoyance.

Star jumped up and barked, standing by the wire of the pen, demanding to be let out. That had been one of Matt's games. Pick things up from the floor and give them to him or to Liz. It always meant high praise and also, quite often, one of her favourite titbits.

Both women turned to stare at her.

She barked again. This was her duty.

'Maybe she needs to go outside,' Sheina said.

She lifted the pen so that Star could come out, but she left the pups behind. Rab had stayed in the annexe with the lambs. He was sure it was his job to guard them.

Sheina opened the door to the yard, but Star ignored it. She walked across the room, picked up the fallen objects, took them one by one in her mouth and laid each in Shelley's lap, making three little journeys. She looked up, her tail waving tentatively, waiting for praise.

It didn't come.

'I don't believe it,' Sheina said, as astonished as her daughter. She set the little table on its legs again. 'Could she have been trained to do that or was it just something to do because she was bored?'

She took one of the pens and dropped it.

This was a game Star always loved. She trotted over, tail waving, picked it up and presented it to Sheina. This time she received the praise she expected, though nobody offered her a titbit. The familiar game excited her and she forgot her fear, looking eagerly at both women, expecting them to continue playing and throw more things for her to fetch.

Neither understood what she needed.

There was a background smell of bacon in the room, although breakfast was long ago. Neither Sheina nor her daughter were aware of it, but Star was. It was a familiar scent among others that she had never met before. It took her back. It triggered another memory.

On summer days Liz and Matt ate breakfast on the patio, Star lying at their feet. There was always bacon. It was a part of her past. It heralded excitement. The postman always called a greeting and handed the little bundle of letters over the gate to Star, who ran to meet him. They were old friends and he always had a goodie for her. This was one of her daily tasks, so long as there was not a parcel too heavy for her to carry.

Her day was punctuated by chores she shared with Matt and Liz. When they cleared the table, Star helped, carrying small unbreakable objects. She observed people closely and then might do something completely unexpected and add it to her other skills.

Star watched the two women. They had stopped talking, and now sat, immersed in their own thoughts. She knew something was wrong. Her need to work overtook her. She could help them. The pups were both awake, sitting like twin bookends, watching in amazement. Houses were new to them and there was so much to see and maybe explore.

Their mother was behaving in a very odd way. They were intrigued.

Greg had left his shoes on the floor near the door, as he had gone out in wellingtons. Star picked them up, one at a time, and took them to Sheina, putting them down neatly side by side at her feet. They stared at her in amazement. They ought to have laughed. Matt always laughed. The dog was puzzled by their reaction.

Dannie's trainers were at the far side of the room, where he had kicked them off to go to bed. Star picked up one of the shoes and put it in Shelley's lap. Perhaps now they would laugh. She needed laughter. It made her feel secure.

Dannie's shoe. Shelley held it, staring at it. Would he ever come back to wear it again? Where was he? She looked at the clock. Half an hour after midnight. She wheeled herself over to the window and lifted the curtain and looked out. The sky had cleared and was a mass of glittering stars. The sight of the white fields and icy yard appalled her. She felt physically sick. Dannie, come home. Please. She would never scold him again. Please, God. She held the shoe tightly, as if it could bring him back to her.

'I think we've found a most unusual dog,' Sheina said, knowing that tears were not far away, and anxious to provide distraction. 'She's trying to tell us something. I'm not sure what.'

Star looked up at them, sensing their distress. Matt and Liz had been unhappy at times, but there had never been a feeling like this. She had almost always succeeded in making them laugh, and then there had been walks in the woods or runs on the beaches, or some new game.

This wasn't happening now. Star wanted results. The dog laid her head on Shelley's lap, offering comfort. There was

56

no change in the sadness that dominated the room, but there was communication. The stroking hands that rewarded her told her she was appreciated.

The kind touch inspired her to keep trying. She looked around. Greg had put his slippers beside his chair. She picked them up, one at a time and offered them to Sheina, looking at her expectantly. Where was her reward?

Shelley cut off a tiny portion of cake, and Star sat, waiting. She took it very gently and then laid her nose on Shelley's hand, looking up at her. Her exertions had tired the dog. She had not quite recovered from the cold and lack of food as she and her pups lay trapped. She flopped at Sheina's feet, her nose on the woman's shoe. Sheina stretched down a hand and stroked the Retriever.

'I suspect we have something special here,' she said. 'Someone must be looking for her. I wonder how on earth she came to be adrift in the hills?'

Outside came Greg's voice, calling.

'Dannie! Dannie!'

There was still no reply.

Nine

Greg whistled to Meg who plodded across to him. She was tiring. It was difficult to walk on snow that, to the dog, was almost knee deep. He patted her head.

'Good lass,' he said. 'We have to find Dannie.'

The prayer resounded in his head. Please God, let us find him. It was a childhood litany. Please God, let everything be all right and I'll never be naughty again. He wished he could remember more about his own childhood. It might help him understand what was going on inside Dannie's head. He felt more and more helpless, anxiety consuming him. What on earth possessed the boy? Especially on a bitterly cold night like this.

He wondered suddenly if Dannie had crept back into the farmhouse and was hiding somewhere there, safe and warm. There were so many rooms, and so many hiding places. Maybe they should have searched there first.

First he'd check the barn, which was the last of the many outbuildings. If Dannie was indoors, he was warm, and safe. Outside . . . the snow was an enemy, covering danger, hiding the deep places, presenting an unbroken smooth surface that might give way to reveal the depths beneath. Depths from which there was no escape.

Suppose the child knew Greg was looking for him and had crept out of one place and into another while his grandfather was elsewhere? Playing some sort of hide and seek? Was Dannie afraid of them? Were they too hard on him? Or were there worse problems at school that the child was afraid to reveal?

He'd search the barn and then the house. Or should he look inside now? Or take out the Land Rover and drive along the road? Was it even passable? The snow lay so deep. For

58

the first time he wished he had a lowland farm and not this place among the bleak mountains where winter was a penance, and snow, for all its beauty, a wicked and unwelcome guest capable of destroying life.

Which should he do first? His thoughts were spinning. Pain knifed through his arthritic knee and he paused to get his breath. He couldn't afford to be out of action now.

He was growing colder by the minute. It was no longer snowing. The temperature had dropped and it was freezing hard. He would have to watch his step. They did not need a man with a broken leg. Dannie could never survive the night in this. There was no chance of a search party.

He had tried the phone again, but it was still dead. In any case, nobody could reach them. They were always cut off in snow. If only it would warm up and thaw. It couldn't last that long in April, could it?

He seemed to be holding an insane conversation with himself. He needed to blot out the vision of his grandson lying frozen. How long did it take to die of hypothermia? Was it quicker for a child? Was he buried in a drift? Or fallen on the ice and lying injured, death a heartbeat away?

He had a sudden unhappy memory of Sheina reading to Dannie a few nights ago. She had found a poem that Shelley had loved as a child. It was about a changeling, stolen away by the fairies. A half-remembered line teased him.

'I shall grow up but never grow old. I will always, always be very cold.'

Dannie had pushed the book away.

'That's silly. Fairyland is lovely and warm. I'd like to go there. It'd be nicer than this.' He had gone across the room to the door and then turned to face them.

'I think I'm a changeling. I wish they'd come and take me back.'

Greg remembered staring at the closed door, wondering how on earth to cope with his small grandson. The child had the oddest thoughts. He needed company of his own age, but not Paul, whoever he was.

Each memory was worse than the last.

When had Dannie left his bed? It was nearly five hours since Shelley had discovered he had gone. The child had been sent to bed two hours before that. If he had run off immediately, those extra hours could spell disaster . . .

The clouds had blown away. The night sky was alive with brilliant stars. The moon, a gleaming silver crescent, gave a shimmering light. A new moon to wish on. It was an absurd relic of his childhood, and a major part of Dannie's. Greg went on praying as he walked, hoping that God would hear him, and would help him find his grandson. Wish upon the moon. Let me find Dannie, alive and well . . . please, please.

Dannie could not have climbed the yard fence, which was high and planted inside with a thick hedge of prickly firethorn. Farms were targets for hunt saboteurs these days. There were two large wooden bins that held logs. He looked inside, but nothing was there but wood.

It seemed ridiculous to waste precious time looking there, but maybe Dannie had gone into the big barn, after all. But why? It seemed most unlikely as the child's fear of the ghost he was sure lived there was almost phobic. Greg had tried to reassure him, insisting the story was nonsense, but nothing he said made any difference. One day the ghost would spring out of the barn and get him. When he first came he was convinced there were tigers on the farm, and they would get him too.

Once Dannie got an idea into his head he stuck with it, and nobody could persuade him that he was wrong. The thoughts circled in Greg's head. Where was he? Why on earth had he decided to run away? Greg did not like to think of a possible reason. There couldn't be one. Had he arranged to meet his friend Paul?

Was it even worth looking in the barn?

Perhaps Paul had dared him to go in there and explore, and bring out a trophy to prove he had been there. It would be on a par with his dare to come to school with spiky red hair. Or was he tormenting the child who had run off to get away from school? Was Dannie being bullied?

Greg's imagination was working overtime. There were so many possibilities, all appalling. Had the child fallen or been injured by some piece of old machinery? He was always fascinated by anything that had an engine. There ought to be a door on the barn, but that had fallen off its hinges long ago.

Dannie had been told repeatedly not to touch things on the farm, but he was intensely curious. He had found a watch in his mother's drawer and taken it apart to see how it worked. Shelley had been angry as it was one of her few mementoes of David, and she had intended to give it to Dannie for his eighteenth birthday. She kept it to treasure. On bad nights she slept with it under her pillow, wanting David back, and life as it had been before the accident. Luckily the watchmaker had been able to put it together again. It was now locked in Greg's own desk.

There were so many other places where a small child might hide, but Greg thought he had explored them all. Dannie would never go in with the pigs, or into the smaller barn where the lambing ewes waited for their time. He avoided the farm animals. He was still a town child in spite of a year in the country. He complained about the smells and the sounds the cattle made, and the sheep.

Greg thrust his hands into his pocket and thanked God for the generator. At least he had light. He pushed the switch. There was no point listening for sounds as the thudding machinery drowned everything else.

The unshaded bulbs revealed a state of disrepair. He came in here only to put the tractor under cover, and was so used to the state of the place that he did not notice the increasing dilapidation. He ought to do something about it. Dannie, when he was older, might be tempted to climb and the place was falling down. Greg was so used to it that he hardly noticed it, but now every corner of the place seemed to reveal a death trap. It was a tip, littered with discarded implements, among them an old plough and his mother's mangle. He must get rid of the ancient machinery. It might fetch a bit at a sale.

There was a sudden flurry of movement as the barn owl swooped down and over Greg's head into the night. Meg barked. Owls had nested there as long as Greg could remember, and were welcome visitors, helping the farm cats keep the rats at bay. Maybe he would get a Jack Russell terrier to help them. Maybe Dannie would take to a pup of his own. Dannie. Dannie.

There were two tractors. The old one served to provide

parts. It stood at the far end of the barn. It was useless. Surely he wouldn't have gone there?

Greg's thoughts chased on around his head.

Meg, behind him, lifted her head and took deep breaths. The generator throbbed noisily, almost deafening him. But at least it enabled him to see. He walked towards the tractor and shouted, hoping he could be heard above the din. He opened the door. Nobody there. But the half dismembered model? It was a remote chance. He almost walked away.

He had to try.

Before he reached it, Meg ran past, stood by the discarded tractor and barked. 'Dannie. Are you there?'

'Grandad.' His voice was faint and choked with sobs. 'I'm in the tractor. The door's stuck.'

Greg pulled open the door and lifted the child out. He was blue with cold, his teeth chattering. He was sobbing, the exhausted sound of a child that had been crying for a long time. He clung to his grandfather with his arms and his legs as if he would never let go.

Greg put him down for a moment, took off his down-filled jacket and wrapped it round the child. Dannie had always been interested in tractors although he had been forbidden to climb on them. An old milking stool beside it showed how he had gained access to the cab.

'Let's go and tell Mummy you're safe.'

'I don't want to see Mummy. She'll be mad with me. Want to be with you and Gran.'

Greg thought the yard had never seemed so vast. He was colder than ever without his jacket. Dannie was heavy. He clung even more tightly to his grandfather, his legs wrapped round him, his sobs subsiding. His teeth chattered and he was shivering as if he could never stop. Greg felt terror overtake him. How long had the child been out there?

He fought the porch door and was thankful at last to reach the kitchen. Rab greeted him as if he had been away for years. Meg, almost too tired to walk, went to her bowl for water, and then flopped on the hearthrug.

Shelley stared at them. She had almost ceased to hope.

'Dannie!'

Her voice broke and she had to struggle to hide tears. She held out her arms. Dannie looked at her and clung more tightly to his grandfather, hiding his face.

Greg settled Dannie in the big chair, where the child was almost lost. He opened the Aga, which cast a warm glow over the big kitchen. Sheina brought her grandson's duvet from his bedroom, and wrapped it round him. She spooned gravy from the casserole into a mug and gave it to the boy to drink.

Slowly the shivering subsided. The colour returned to his face. He was too tired to react when they spoke to him and twenty minutes after he had finished his soup he was asleep.

'Put him in my bed,' Sheina said. 'I'll sleep in his. Then if he wakes up you'll be there beside him. It's going to take a long time for him to get over this.'

Rab and Meg were back in the annexe and Sheina had put Star in the pen with her pups when Greg came in. Dannie had been too tired to notice them.

Greg lifted him, and carried him upstairs. He undressed the child, who didn't even wake, and tucked him into one of the twin beds. Bruises on his arms and legs stood out starkly against the chilled skin. Greg studied them in dismay. Had the boy knocked himself about in the tractor, or were they signs of some earlier trauma? He was glad to stretch out himself and get warm. He left the landing light on, so that Dannie would not wake up to darkness.

Downstairs Sheina tidied the kitchen. She was exhausted. It was nearly four a.m. She let the dogs out for the last time, taking Star on a lead lest she raced off. Shelley did not speak. She knew that once alone she would start to cry and felt as if that happened she would never stop. Sheina ached as she looked at her daughter. She helped her into bed.

'Mum, he hates me.'

'It'll be different tomorrow,' Sheina said, trying to believe her own words. 'He's tired and upset. He's a very mixed-up little boy.'

'We were so happy,' Shelley said. She had to confess. 'It was so stupid . . . one mistake. I should have driven that night. I didn't know David had had a couple of double whiskies while I was in the cloak room. He was so excited

63

about his new job. I'd had enough wine to make me reckless. I just didn't think. It's all my fault.'

The tears came at last. Sheina sat on the bed, holding her daughter as she had held her when she was a little girl. It was the first time Shelley had allowed her mother to hug her since she came home. It was the first time she had spoken of the accident, or of David's irresponsibility.

Sheina left her at last. Greg had put her night clothes on Dannie's bed. Nearly five o'clock and she had to be up early to feed the lambs and milk Toffee. There was extra work with the refugee and her pups.

It was a long time before she slept.

Dannie cried out in his sleep, waking his grandfather. The ghost had come to get him, swooping down from the sky and he couldn't run away. His legs had locked. The cry turned into a scream. He woke. He was in a strange bed and an unfamiliar room, but the landing light showed him that he was with Grandad.

Greg woke at once and was out of bed, holding the child closely to him.

'It's all right, Dannie. Nothing can hurt you now. You're safe.'

Dannie gripped his grandfather's hand.

'Can I come into your bed? I want a cuddle.'

Greg held him tightly, knowing the child needed human contact. He glanced at the clock. Six a.m. Sheina had given up all thoughts of sleep and was moving about downstairs. She would have fed the lambs, and seen to the dogs. A few more minutes would not hurt.

'What did you dream?' Greg asked, as the child relaxed. He looked up sleepily.

'The ghost was coming to get me. I couldn't move. It was horrible, out there in the dark. I called you but you didn't come.'

'We couldn't hear you,' Greg said, thinking of those lonely hours. 'Dannie, why did you go into the barn?'

Dannie had had a long time on his own, time to be afraid, to be sure nobody would find him for days and days and days and then he'd be dead of hunger and thirst and cold. Now he was with Grandad in the warm, and Grandad was looking at him with worry in his eyes. Dannie knew he could trust him.

Suddenly he needed to confide things he had been keeping secret. Secret because Paul told him terrible things would happen to him if he told, and he, Paul would do them. And Paul would, Dannie knew.

Maybe Grandad would help him. Maybe it was better to tell.

'I was going to meet Paul. His dad was taking him to London and he said his dad would take me too so I could see my dad. I know where we lived and he'll still be there. Only it began to snow and Paul wasn't there and it was hard to walk and I didn't know which way he'd come and it was cold and I didn't want to go home as Mummy would only be cross.'

Greg was appalled. If only Dannie had told them what was happening.

'I was coming back to the house past the big barn when the ghost came. He came across the yard and I knew he was trying to get me so I ran. Only I didn't notice I was running to the barn and he came after me, and I thought it would be safe and warm in the tractor and I could get out in the morning.'

He took another deep breath which ended in a sob.

'I tried to get into the big tractor but I couldn't open the door. Then the ghost came down towards me again. I ran to the old tractor and the door opened and I got inside so the ghost couldn't catch me and then when I shut it it wouldn't open again. I thought maybe I could open it in the morning. I couldn't see. Ghosts only come at night. Only it wasn't warm and there were horrid noises, and . . .'

Tears came again. Greg held him tightly, till the storm had passed. The child was shivering and his teeth were chattering. Greg found it hard to hide his dismay.

'Dannie. There are no ghosts. What was the ghost like?'

'An enormous bird. It was all white and it didn't make any noise at all. It just chased me.'

'Dannie, that was the owl. He was going back to his nest. He's a big bird and he never makes a noise. You can't even hear his wings. You were near his babies and he didn't like it.'

'It was a ghost,' Dannie said. 'They can take any shape they like. And then it made a noise like thunder.'

He began to shake again. He had never been so frightened in his life, huddling there in the dark. It had become much worse when the generator started thumping, sounding as if it were almost on top of him. He didn't know where the noise came from as it had never been needed before. He thought there was another ghost out there, this one a giant, whose thundering footsteps were shaking the ground, coming for him.

The electricity had been connected to the main grid just before Dannie came to live with his grandparents. This was the first power cut since then.

Greg felt guilt overwhelm him. None of them had enough time for the child. They were always so busy. When Dannie talked Greg knew that, when he was tired, he only half listened, making soothing noises, but not conversing at all.

There was too much to do on the farm. Far too much for two people. They never had time to rest, or to sit down and relax. Nothing was easy. Any improvements he made were for Shelley's benefit. There was no way he would use her life insurance money for the farm's needs. That was for Dannie. Children grew up fast, and one day there would be university fees.

He could hear Sheina moving downstairs. Time to get up and help her.

'Go and wash, Dannie. Then dress. Have your breakfast and then we'll go and see your mum.'

Shelley had her breakfast in bed and then Sheina helped her wash and dress. Would Dannie go and see her? Somehow they had to convince the child that everything Paul had told him was nonsense.

And that was going to be very difficult indeed.

Ten

Downstairs, Greg waited for his grandson. He had slept little in what remained of the night, and spent most of the time thinking. Time to involve Dannie in the farm. Time somehow to make sure the child enjoyed his life. Maybe the school was right and Dannie should see a psychologist. It was not a thought that pleased Greg.

Dannie came into the room, walking hesitantly, as if afraid that he might be told off. Running away was wicked. Bad children ran away. Paul had said they'd be on the corner of the lane, but they hadn't come.

Greg decided to start involving his grandson now.

'Maybe Black Henny will have laid you an egg. Come with me to find it? Would you like to have it today?'

Normally Dannie would have avoided the hen run, but he needed to be as near his grandfather as was possible. He didn't want him out of his sight. The ghosts might come back if he were alone. Besides, Black Henny's eggs were special: brown and very big and they often had double yolks. Grandad always had them because Gran said they were too big for a little boy. This was a real treat.

The weather had changed overnight. Outside, when Sheina drew back the curtains, the yard was almost free of snow. It lay in the gullies at the edges and in patches in the fields. There was snow on the high hills, the sun gilding the tops. The snowman was half size, his face a ruin, his hat now on the ground where the wind had blown it.

Dannie did not venture into the hen run, but he took the brown egg from his grandfather. He loved boiled eggs.

'It's warm,' he said.

'She's just laid it. Let's take it to Gran and I'll make soldiers.'

67

Dannie was eager to get back to the kitchen and he was hungry.

'Don't run,' Greg said. 'If you fall there won't be any egg. You must walk slowly and carefully as you are holding something very precious that might break.'

Sheina, busy making breakfast for all of them, smiled when Dannie handed her the egg.

'I think Henny laid it specially for you,' she said. 'Four minutes and then up to the table.'

Dannie did not hear her. He was staring at the pen, at the three golden dogs lying inside, two of them tinier than any dog he had ever seen. He had barely noticed them last night. He had been so cold and so tired. Star came to the wire, her tail wagging, when he walked over to look at them more closely.

'Where did they come from? They're not ours.'

'I found them under the snow on the hill when Meg and I were looking for sheep,' Greg said. 'They were even colder than you were.'

Dannie looked at the dogs thoughtfully. He was not at all sure that he liked them. Still, at least they didn't bark at him. The pups began to play, and he stood, watching, entertained by their antics.

'Food,' Sheina said. 'I'm taking your mum her breakfast. She was very worried indeed about you and she isn't feeling very well today. She couldn't sleep. We'll go and see her when you've eaten your egg.'

Dannie said nothing. If he went to see his mum she'd be angry and shout at him. He wondered why she'd worried. She didn't really want him. Paul said so. Paul said she didn't want him or his dad and that was why she had sent his dad away. That's what Paul's mum had done and she didn't really want Paul either only the judge said Paul had to live with her.

Dannie couldn't understand why the judge had to decide where Paul lived. Maybe he'd understand next year when he was seven. By then Paul would be eight so he'd know even more. Dannie gave up. He was too hungry.

He took his place at the table. His grandfather had a big plate of bacon and eggs and black pudding, but Dannie's thoughts were on his own special egg. The two slices of toast were cut into fingers. Soldiers. He only had those on special days.

Eating took priority. He hoped Gran had forgotten that they were going to see his mum and there were other chores to be done. Memory of the cold floor of the tractor suddenly overwhelmed him, and he looked round the kitchen.

For the first time it felt like home, with the big Aga and the shabby old chairs beside it. His mum's cushion covers brightened the place. By the time he had finished his breakfast Gran was with his mother. He joined his grandfather in the annexe. No school today as it was Saturday.

The pups needed feeding, as did the lambs. For the first time since he had come to live with them Dannie agreed to help. Paul said helping his grandparents wasn't cool. But Paul wasn't here. Paul hadn't come looking for him and carried on till he found him. Grandad had done that. Gran said they had been hunting for him for hours. He had heard Greg calling and had answered but his voice didn't carry. He couldn't open the tractor door and even if he could, he was too afraid of the ghost to venture outside.

He didn't want to remember. He immersed himself in the small jobs he could do.

He fed two of the lambs, surprised by their energy as they almost pulled the teat off the bottle in their eagerness. Greg welcomed his laughter but suspected his cooperation was due to Dannie's desire not to meet his mother yet, rather than eagerness to help. The child was subdued, and did as he was asked without arguing.

There was little to be done today and Greg could afford to relax. He made coffee for himself. Dannie wanted fruit juice.

He looked up at his grandfather.

'Will you take me to London to see my Dad?' he asked.

Greg did not know how to answer. How did he make his grandson understand that David really was dead? He would have to see if the Head could do something about Paul, but should you break up a friendship? And could you? How could they be kept apart? The other child probably did not understand that Dannie really had lost his father.

69

Dannie never mentioned the car crash.

Racking his brains, Greg remembered his wife's cuttings book. She always kept any reference to the family. Engagement announcements, wedding announcements, Shelley's exam results. Pictures of their daughter when she won in local showjumping events. She and the vet's son Jamie had been rivals when they were both in the pony club.

There were also pictures of Greg's grandfather, of his father and of Greg himself with winning animals, and with various dignitaries and members of the royal family presenting the trophy. The local papers gave good coverage to anyone living in their area. The farm featured prominently as so many of their beasts won prizes at the Agricultural Shows.

But had Sheina kept the reports of the accident? Or was that too traumatic?

'Have you ever seen your gran's family history book?'

Dannie shook his head.

'She says when I'm an extra very very good boy,' he said. 'She always puts it away when I come 'cos she says my fingers aren't clever enough to turn it over without tearing. Bits of it are very old. My mum doesn't like looking at it. She says she doesn't want to remember.'

Sheina had taken Star out of the pen to exercise in the yard. They came in through the door. Star went at once to the pen and nosed her two pups. Then she turned to look at Dannie, knowing that he lived here too. His scent was every-where. She walked over to him and licked his hand.

'She's not a collie,' Dannie said. 'She's not a farm dog. Are you going to keep her?'

'Someone might be looking for her,' Greg said. 'We'll see. She seems quite at home here for the moment.'

Star settled on the rug, lying against the pen.

Greg took the scrapbook from the dresser drawer and began to turn the pages.

'We bred Shires then, Dannie,' Greg said, pointing to a picture of their best stallion, who was overall champion and was at the Horse of the Year Show. He was in his prime, decorated with ribbons and horse brasses.

'His name was Majestic Sunrise. My dad bred his sire. That's the horse's dad. His name was Supreme Majesty. His

70

mum, Sunrise Treasure, was one of our top prize winners.'

'They're big,' Dannie said. 'Who's that on the horse's back?

Greg laughed.

'That's me. I was three years old when Sunrise became a champion. There was a party to celebrate and I was allowed to stay up. I loved being lifted on to Sunny's back and looking down on all the people who always looked down on me.'

Great-gran's memory book, Shelley called it. She loved cuddling up to him as a little girl and hearing about all the animals that were featured. His grandmother had started it.

'That's my great-grandad getting a cup from King Edward the Seventh; and that's my grandad getting one from George the Fifth . . . and there's my father getting another from Prince Philip.'

Dannie was beginning to be intrigued.

'And that's me getting a cup from the Queen when our bull was Supreme Champion. She's a lovely lady. She said she thought he was a grand beast.'

He sighed. That had indeed been a day to remember.

No time for any of that now. It had been such fun. Those growing up now missed so much, but would never know it.

He had found the huge file of cuttings after his mother died. She always meant to paste them into a scrap book to make them easier to read, but never got round to it. Sheina was fascinated and began it in the last month of her pregnancy. Plenty of time then with four men working here, Greg thought, regretting the old days. Grandad and Dad and me, as well as the extra hands. It's difficult to realize how much life has changed.

He turned another page.

'That's Emperor dressed for the 1934 May Day parade. I hadn't been born then but the horse lived to thirty and was part of my growing up. We had such fun with the horses, Dannie. On May the first we always had a splendid celebration. Every horse and pony in the district was dressed up and all the carts were decorated.'

'Don't they do it now?' Dannie asked.

'Sadly, no. Look, this is Daybreak. She won the prize for

the best turned-out mare. Doesn't she look fantastic? We didn't have colour cameras then. All those ribbons in their manes and tails were such bright colours and the brasses were cleaned till they shone.'

The book brought back so many memories. Life had seemed so much easier then, in spite of the lack of technology. Now machines did everything . . . and broke down. Or there was a power failure.

'I wish they still celebrated May Day with the horses,' he said. 'You'd have loved it all. The parades came back briefly after the war, and there were even maypoles in some places. The brasses had to be polished till they gleamed like sunlight. All those bright ribbons had to be braided. The men spent hours on them. They stayed up all night to groom and clean the white feathering till it shone like silken snow.'

He sat, turning the pages, looking back through the years.

Sheina had kept the cuttings about the crash in which David was killed. Greg knew that the child would be upset to read them but it was surely better for him to realize they were telling him the truth than for him to go on thinking that his father was still alive and had abandoned him, or that his mother had thrust him out of their lives.

'That's your name,' Dannie said, looking out a small paragraph at the top of the page.

'My dad,' Greg said, looking over his shoulder. 'Your great-grandad. That was after he died.'

It read:

MCLEOD. Gregory and Sheina and the family of the late Donald McLeod wish to thank everybody for the cards, letters, phone calls and visits to them expressing sympathy at their loss. We also wish to thank those who cared for him, and the many donations which enabled us to present a cheque for £1000 to the St Agnes' Hospice as a tangible token of our appreciation.

'Why did you write that?' Dannie asked.

'Grandad had cancer and was ill for a long time. A lot of people were very kind to him. Too many to write and thank so we put it in the paper so everyone could read it and know that we were grateful to them.'

Dannie turned over the pages.

'A lot of people died,' he said.

Sheina had started a new section for Shelley, beginning with the announcement of her birth. There were paragraphs on her wins at the Pony Club events, on her degree, her engagement and wedding notices.

'To Shelley and David Barham, a son, Daniel Gregory.'

'That's me,' Dannie shouted. 'I'm Daniel Gregory Barham.'

There was nothing else on that page and then on the next page a notice caught his eyes. He looked at it for a long time. Greg watched him, wondering if he were doing right.

The newspaper caption read DEATHS.

Below it was the stark little paragraph, dated thirteen months ago.

BARHAM. David John, son of Lois and John Barham, husband of Shelley and father of Daniel. Suddenly, as the result of an accident. Funeral on March 14th at Sunholt Parish Church, followed by cremation at Danton Crematorium. Family flowers only. Donations to Lanton Children's Hospice.

Greg wondered what the child was thinking. There was a long silence, as Dannie absorbed the words. At last he gave a deep sigh.

'Why did Paul say my Dad was alive?'

'Paul doesn't know,' Greg said. 'I expect he thinks everyone's the same as he is. He's obviously a very unhappy little boy who misses his own Dad terribly.'

'Why wasn't Daddy's funeral here?'

'Nobody here really knew him,' Greg said. 'He and your mummy didn't live here after they were married. His funeral was in the place where he lived all his life with his mother and father. Everyone knew him there. '

'What's cremation?' Dannie asked, looking at the paragraph again.

'Do you remember when Polly died last year?' Greg asked.

Polly had been Sheina's special dog for fourteen years.

'Yes, Gran asked for her ashes. And then we took them and shook them where she always played. So she's always round us.'

'Your dad's ashes were taken to the Lake District where he loved climbing,' Greg said. 'We're going to put a memorial plaque in the church here for him, so you and Mummy have that to remember. Only we haven't been able to arrange it yet. I wanted to wait a little while, till Mummy begins to feel better.'

'So Mummy didn't send daddy away?'

'No, Dannie. They were having a celebration. Your daddy had a new job. That's why they went out and left you with Christine. He wanted to have a party, just the two of them.' He sighed. 'They did have their party. The accident happened on the way home. Your daddy died. Mummy was very badly hurt. You know that.'

'Paul said she was making it up 'cos she's lazy and likes people to do all her work for her. She stayed away 'cos she didn't want me. She wasn't in hospital. You just told me that to make it sound better. She was having fun without me or my Dad.'

'None of that's true.' Greg felt desperate. 'Paul says a lot of things that are very silly indeed.'

He was angry. How could one child make life so impossible for so many people? What sort of child was he? What could they do about him? Something must be done and fast. On Monday he would go and see the Headmistress.

The door opened and Sheina came in, followed by Star, who had been let out into the yard. The dog came straight up to Dannie and put her head on his knee.

Dannie looked at her. Brown eyes looked back at him.

'She knows I'm sad,' he said.

At that moment the phone rang. It triggered Star's memory. She trotted across the floor and took it from its cradle. She turned, as if working out who would need it and then brought it to Greg who watched her in astonishment, wondering if the noise upset her and she intended to demolish it.

She pushed the phone into his hands, releasing it the second she was sure that he held it firmly.

74

'Clever girl,' he said, enthusiasm in his voice. 'Now that's very interesting indeed. I wonder what else she's been taught? She could prove to be the answer to all our problems. I wish you could talk, girl, and tell us what you do know.'

'She needs a name,' Sheina said. 'I wonder what she has been called? I don't suppose we'll ever guess. What shall we call her, Dannie?'

'What about Hope?' Greg asked. 'I think she could give that to us all.'

'Why?' Dannie asked.

Greg smiled but did not answer.

Eleven

Dannie had a lot to think about. Every idea he had seemed to have been stood on its head. He had been so cold and so frightened the night before. His grandfather had been security and safety, bringing him out of the icy black pit he seemed to be inhabiting into warmth and the rejoicing of his mother and grandmother when they found he was safe.

Grandad had spent hours looking for him, had held him tightly, murmuring to him, had brought him into the warm kitchen with familiar objects round him. He was suddenly aware that the familiar routine in which he refused to take part was a comfort in itself. Arms hugged him. He seemed to be waking from a very bad dream.

Star seemed to sense his need, and leaned against him, head on his knees, watching him. Her brown eyes were so gentle. Paul said it wasn't cool to farm and only soppy people liked animals. Tough people knew that they were icky wicky sicky. Paul liked pulling kittens' tails. And kicking them. Not cats, as they scratched, but a tiny kitten was helpless.

They had found one one day, behind the school bicycle sheds. No one was about. Dannie watched, feeling sick. He refused to take part. And then Paul hit him instead of the kitten, which ran away, hopefully to find safety and recover.

Dannie felt very bad about that. Why hadn't he told anyone? It was stupid. Why had he wanted to impress Paul so much?

He shivered. He knew that answer. Because Paul's kindness had to be won. If it wasn't then Dannie had to be punished and the older boy was both imaginative and subtle. Nobody would ever guess what Paul was really like except those he used to satisfy his own needs. Dannie sensed this but could never have put it into words.

He had questions to ask his mother and grandfather.

'Did Daddy die in the car?' he asked. 'He didn't go to hospital to be made better?'

Greg didn't know how to soften the news.

'He was too badly hurt, Dannie.'

'I thought he was at home. In London. Without us. That was what Paul said. I thought that Mummy didn't want to see him any more. Like Paul's mum. She hates his dad. They never meet, not even when he comes for Paul. Paul says his dad takes him to the cinema and to aeroplane landing fields and to fancy restaurants but his mummy never takes him anywhere. She doesn't want Paul either. But she won't let him go to his dad all the time.'

Neither had seen Shelley come into the room.

'Paul said Mummy's either bone idle and useless or she drinks too much. That's why she can't walk, because if she did she'd fall over. Drunks don't love people. They only love drinking.'

Shelley stared at Dannie. His words had shocked her out of her apathy. All these months she had been grieving for David, forgetting Dannie had loved his father too. She had been lost in her conviction that she had been instrumental in her husband's death. That conviction plagued her in the long, sleepless, pain-filled nights. Why hadn't she insisted that she drove? Why had she had even those two glasses of wine, sure they wouldn't affect her? She could think of little else.

That lapse of judgement haunted her.

All through the year her thoughts had been on herself. Dannie was there, in the background, but she had been too obsessed to realize how much his father's loss affected him. And she hadn't been there for him either. Only her parents had, as they tried desperately to comfort a child they barely knew.

Dannie's words roused her, so that she longed to reach out to him, to hold him. He had been so difficult since she came home, as if determined to make himself unlovable. Nothing like the bright happy child she remembered. She had been too unhappy to even try to understand. She had failed Dannie as well as David.

77

How on earth could the child believe such an idea? As realization dawned, she felt a wave of anger flooding her, bringing her back to life. Numbed feelings flared into pain. She nerved herself, not sure what she was going to say.

Greg saw her, but put his finger to his lips. Better to say nothing for now. Better to let the child assimilate the truth, and think about it.

Dannie was running his fingers over the paper, as if he could absorb comfort through them. He wanted to cry but he hurt too much to cry. Big boys don't cry. His father had said so. His father wasn't there any more.

Never would be there again. All these months Dannie had cherished the thought that one day he would go back to London, and live in the house where he had lived since he was born. Hear his father's voice and hear his key in the door. Run to him to be lifted as he had been when he was little, and swung high in the air with a laughing shout of 'How's my boy then?'

Shelley watched her son, aching for him, wondering what was going through his mind. If only she had been here for him instead of lying useless in the hospital so far away. Life dealt some very nasty blows at times. For the first time, misery was compounded by anger. The anger roused her.

She had sat back too long, had relied on others too long. It was time to take responsibility for herself and Dannie. Time to do more than sit drowning in self pity.

'Your life isn't over,' the doctor at the hospital had said. 'You might have lost the use of your legs. You haven't lost your wits. It'll take time. It'll be a challenge. It's up to you.'

Easy for him, she thought then. She was aware of the ticking clock, of a mew as the cat came in through the flap, saw Star and went out again. Star went over to the wheelchair, sensing that she was needed. Shelley put out a hand to stroke the soft fur, to gain comfort from the trusting head on her knee.

Greg said nothing, giving the boy a chance to assimilate what he had been told. He had big adjustments to make.

Shelley sighed. Dannie was so like his father in appearance. The blonde hair that had a cockscomb at the back that would never lie flat. The brown eyes that could look so

78

reproachful. The curve of his cheek and his lips and long lashes were hers, but he would be tall like David, probably taller than his grandfather.

Was he like his father in character? She tightened her hold on Star, who moved restlessly, disliking restraint. The dog looked up at her, brown eyes asking for a gentler grip. The appeal had its effect. Shelley stroked the soft fur. This creature too had suffered. Any fool could see she had been carefully reared, brilliantly trained and that the last weeks must have been hell for her. Shelley hoped, suddenly and desperately, that Star would not be claimed. She needed the dog.

There was a comfort in animals that humans could not give. She had not allowed herself to remember that.

Shelley looked at Dannie as if she had never seen him before. She wondered what he was thinking, and whether now they might find a rapport. She had lost the bond with her son.

She felt that they had grown so far apart that they might never even be friends. It was her fault. All of it. From the moment she let David take the car keys from her and hadn't protested.

'I'm fine,' he had said. 'Don't fuss. Come on. Christine needs to get home.'

Their babysitter lived five doors away. Her mother was always at the end of the phone if Christine were worried, and it only took a few minutes to reach their house.

It hadn't been fine. David was inclined to be reckless even when sober. He had been well over the limit. The car in front of them was too slow and he was always impatient. She saw the approaching lorry as he overtook. Everything seemed to happen in slow motion. There was nothing she could do. There was nowhere to go. She could still hear the crash of metal, feel the shock. Knowing that her legs were trapped and she couldn't move. Knowing that David was dead.

She could still hear the cutting tools that took the roof off to free them. Those endless minutes played in her head, a relentless sequence. They haunted her dreams.

Her in-laws brought Dannie to see her, just once, but he was terrified by the unfamiliar figure in the bed, the bandages round her head and the tubes that helped her to breathe.

She had only been half conscious. But she had been aware of him and of his screams when he saw her.

'That's not my mummy. Where's my daddy?'

Sheina arrived the next day, and sat, holding her daughter's hand, tears sliding down her cheeks. Shelley knew she was there, but was unable to speak, able only to twitch her fingers. It had been weeks before any sensation came back into her arms. Dannie went back with his grandmother to Scotland. Much too far away for any visits.

Her in-laws came once a week, bringing flowers and grapes and uneasy conversation. 'You'll be fine. Give it time.' She was sure they blamed her for David's death. They did their duty, but she knew there was no real affection. She was the mother of their grandson. She spoke to Dannie on the phone, but he had little to say.

She felt isolated, cut off from daily life, trapped in her hospital bed, needing the services of nurses to help her with the most mundane of tasks. She hated her dependency on others. She wanted David and cried out for him in her dreams.

She envied the nurses who could walk, run, laugh, talk, go away from the hospital into the real world while she was trapped like an animal in a cage.

There were small achievements. As the use of her arms returned she could brush her own hair, feed herself, and wash her face and hands. Sheina sent little parcels of make up, of perfume and talc. There were pictures from Dannie, and Shelley wrote to him, having to learn to write all over again. She had little to say.

She could put a brave face on each day. She had been too dispirited to try for her old job again, too much in need of her family's support to stay in London, but when the occupational therapist discovered that Shelley had been a designer for a fashion house and loved embroidery she had brought her materials to work on.

She made Dannie a Shire horse. She wrapped it herself and sent it with a letter on his sixth birthday. When she came home she had found it in the bottom drawer of the chest in his room, still wrapped in tissue paper, obviously never touched. She took it out and held it and cried into its soft velvet body.

Dannie had needed her and she hadn't been there, and in these months at home nothing had been easy. Her back always hurt. She tired so easily. Though Sheina helped her a lot, she had more to do than she had in the hospital as she insisted on trying to take a share of the indoor work.

She could cook, load the dishwasher, prepare vegetables, feed the lambs. Greg offered to take her shopping but she couldn't face the world yet. A world of people who either stared at her or pretended she wasn't there. Who didn't know how to treat her. It was worse for those who had known her before.

Shelley wished she could switch off her thoughts.

Dannie was still silent. His mother made coffee for herself and her parents. It was something to do. The last born lamb was a weakling and Sheina was feeding him every two hours. She was busy in the annexe. Shelley poured fruit juice into a glass.

Greg took a beaker of coffee through to his wife. On the way back he picked up his own mug and Dannie's glass. He wished he could think of words that would help, could break the silence, which seemed to go on for ever. What was Dannie thinking? On top of everything else, the boy had to re-evaluate his friendship with Paul, who had so misled him.

Was that deliberate, a desire to hurt Dannie and make mischief, or did the child genuinely believe that Dannie's home situation was identical to his? Greg did not have to wonder what Shelley thought. The expression on her face hurt him. He longed to hug her, to comfort her, to murmur to her as he had when she was tiny and had cut her knee or suffered some other childish woe.

There were times even then when nobody could comfort her and she had to learn to handle her own suffering. The day her pony was so ill the vet came for the last time. She cried herself to sleep for a month. She was two years older than Dannie was now. Bracken had been part of her life for seven years, bought when she was only one year old.

She could never bear to lose a dog or cat. He doubted if she was any tougher now. Maybe less so. Her helplessness had made her more vulnerable. Yet even when tiny she had been independent. Let me do it. I can do it. Don't help me. I'm not a baby.

Now she was insisting that she was part of the household and contributed her share. She needed encouragement but she was trying too hard, too soon, and exhausting herself, with an inevitable slide into despair. She railed at Sheina if she did any job that Shelley could manage.

'I'm not an invalid. Don't treat me like one.'

Dannie got down from his chair and went to his bedroom. He came back a few minutes later with his parents' wedding photograph and put it on the dresser.

'I hid it because I thought you didn't love Daddy any more,' he told his mother. He did not look at her while he was speaking.

Shelley looked at the picture. Herself in white, looking up at David with adoration in her eyes. David in the morning suit he had grumbled so much about but finally worn, laughing down at her.

She couldn't answer Dannie. If she did the tears would flood again and she didn't want him to see her crying.

Star was watching these new people. They were as pleased when she brought the phone to them as Matt and Liz had been. There were other things she could do. She wanted to change the atmosphere, which worried her. If she could make them laugh . . . that had always worked with Liz and Matt.

She sat in front of Greg, expectant, and barked just once, asking him to give her some occupation. That was how she and Matt had communicated and that bark was the signal for one of their many games. Greg thought that she needed to go outside and he opened the back door. She stared up at him in puzzlement, refusing to move. She was seated beside Greg's chair. She barked again. Why couldn't they see what she wanted?

Both Dannie and Shelley were distracted by the dog's behaviour. It was good to have something else to focus on. We need time to adjust, Shelley thought. Time for Dannie to understand what's true and what isn't.

There were footsteps outside, and the dogs barked. The letter box rattled as two letters fell through. Star, seeing them, ran across the room, picked them up and offered them to Greg.

His curiosity was aroused. He had worked with dogs all

his life, but this one was acting in a way he had not met before. He was sure she knew exactly what she was doing. Someone had taught her to a high degree. If she had been trained in the way he suspected she would be a godsend for Shelley and might intrigue Dannie too. The child needed distraction.

How to find out?

Twelve

Star was feeling much better. It would take time to put weight back on her, but she was no longer ravenous and she had no need to hunt. Her eager eyes watched every move that these new humans made.

They were asking her to do things that were familiar.

Greg picked up a pen from the big old fashioned dresser and dropped it on the floor. That was a favourite game. She had often played it with Matt. It gave her a feeling of security.

No use using her new name yet, Greg thought. Hope. It was as good as any other and nothing like Rab or Meg so there would be no confusion. She would have to learn it. She responded to hand signals. He pointed to the pen.

'Fetch it, lass,' he said. She did not need telling what to do. She knew what 'fetch it' meant, though 'lass' was a new word to her. It did not change the meaning, though. The use of her skills excited her. She had done this before, so often. She trotted across the floor, picked it up easily and returned to him, offering it for him to take. Her eyes watched him, trusting him, expecting praise, but she was surprised by his enthusiasm.

That was what Matt did when she had learned something new. This was routine, but she savoured the different approach. She waved her tail, then looked around the room for something else she could do. The metal water bowl was empty. She was thirsty. She brought it to Greg, and banged it down on his knees. He laughed and filled it for her.

'She's telling me off,' he said. 'I ought to have noticed. Isn't she clever?'

Star, having almost emptied the bowl, settled on the hearthrug, nose on paws, watching. She was ready to leap up at a signal, to do whatever was wanted. Dannie was now sitting in the big chair, his knees up to his chest, his arms round them and his hands linked. He watched, fascinated. Meg and Rab didn't do things like this.

'What else can she do?' he asked.

'If I'm right, she can do a lot of things,' his grandfather said. 'We'll let her rest for a little while.'

Dannie had a lot to think about. Paul had been wrong about his dad. And his mum. Maybe he was wrong about aliens too. And other things. He remembered huddling in the icy cold cab of the tractor and shivered. That was Paul's fault too. Greg saw the shiver and wondered if there was psychological harm from the child's escapade. He did not know how to deal with that.

Also, Dannie had now to accept the fact that his father really was dead. It must have been easier for him to think David was still alive but living somewhere else. There was always the hope then that they would meet again.

Star nosed his knee, impatient. Perhaps the dog could do even more. She was almost a circus act, and Dannie was enchanted. Greg racked his brains.

'Sit very still and don't say anything,' he told his grandson. 'Let's try and find out what she does know.'

Star watched him, eager to discover what he wanted. This was what she had been born for. This was what she needed.

Greg produced shoes, slippers, Sheina's peg bag, a rolled-up junk mail magazine that had come through the post the day before and not been opened, and a variety of odd objects that he put on the floor. He only had to point and Star brought them to him. She knew the names of many of them.

He ran out of ideas. Star looked around. The car keys were on a side table. She picked them up and stood, thoughtful. She remembered something that had amused Matt and Liz. She carried them across the room and dropped them in her water bowl.

She was rewarded by the laughter that followed.

'Hey, lass. That won't do. Bring them to me,' Greg said, and held out his hand. Star retrieved them, shook them, and brought them back to him.

'Wow! I didn't know you could teach a dog to do things like that,' Dannie said. He had a sudden vision of himself telling his schoolmates about this miracle dog, better than any dog he'd seen on the telly. Not like Meg and Rab, who just herded sheep.

Maybe they'd take more notice of him now. Paul couldn't produce anything to cap that.

'Do you think there's anything else she can do?'

Sheina had come in for her coffee and was watching. Meg and Rab were watching too.

'Lie down,' he told them. They dropped obediently, lying side by side. The pups were also watching their mother.

He thought the collies looked somewhat bemused. No dog they had ever seen behaved like this. Maybe she could also be taught to herd and he could give Meg a well-earned rest, only taking her out on easy jobs. He could still use her to herd close to the farm. She'd hate to be retired.

Star looked round for something else to do. Then she saw another familiar object. She went across the room and sat in front of the tumbler drier, staring at it intently. Greg, intrigued, remembered a dog he had seen working on TV, helping a disabled woman. He opened the door. The dry clothes from yesterday were waiting to be put into the laundry basket to carry upstairs and put away; Dannie's escapade had interrupted their routine.

He picked up the basket from the corner where it stood and set it down in front of the dog.

Very gently, she took each article out and dropped it into the basket.

'Wow! She's a miracle,' an excited voice said from the doorway. 'She'd be a godsend. She could do so much for Shelley and I bet you could teach her to hold a bottle and feed a lamb, to save you time. I've seen a collie do that.'

Greg, startled, turned round to see Jamie just inside the room. He had been so engrossed that he hadn't heard the young vet come in.

'I've been watching. Someone's lost a good dog,' Jamie said. 'She's incredible.'

He looked thoughtfully at Star, who had lifted her head,

86

staring at him, as if wondering if he were a safe person to allow into the house.

'I wasn't expecting you.' Greg, his mind on large vet bills, was somewhat worried by this unexpected visit. 'Rab's paw is healing? It's not infected?'

'The antibiotics have taken care of that. It's fine. Sheina rang,' Jamie said. 'Didn't she tell you? She wanted me to check this bitch and the pups and also make sure Toffee's recovered. I was passing anyway. Been up all night at Jimmie McCann's. Cow with a bad calving.'

'Is she OK?' Greg asked, knowing that her loss would be a small disaster.

'Fine. Nice little heifer. But we had a struggle.'

He stroked Meg, who was one of his favourites and had come to greet him. Star watched her. She did not yet know this man, but if Meg accepted him then she would.

Jamie took his favourite perch on the edge of the big table.

'I'm glad the snow's gone. If it hadn't there'd be a number of animals in trouble.'

'It had me scared,' Greg said. He didn't want to mention Dannie's escapade in front of the child. He didn't want to live through a night like that again. 'I'll be glad when Toffee's better,' he said instead, glad to have something else to think about. He could cope with animals. They were predictable and very rewarding, unlike small boys. He wondered if that was the real problem. They had only had a daughter. As far as he could see from friends with families, small girls were more biddable until their teens. Boys were rebels as soon as they could walk. Full of adventure and curiosity.

He brought his thoughts back to the present. 'Shelley went through a phase of not liking cow's milk, though,' he said. 'I had to make an extra journey each day to get goat's milk from the Thomases. Now she's decided she doesn't like that instead.'

'I don't like goat's milk either,' Dannie said.

'Tell you a secret,' Jamie said. 'I don't either, but don't tell your grandad.'

Dannie looked up at Greg, who was grinning.

Jamie looked down at Star.

'I think I'd better ring the people who deal with dogs for

the disabled when I get home,' he said. 'Just to make sure none of their clients has a missing animal. This is a very highly trained dog.'

'I'll be praying nobody has lost one,' Greg said.

Jamie was already making plans. 'Maybe having the dog as companion would help Shelley come to terms with what's happened. There's such a lot she still can do, if only she'd realize it.'

He sighed, remembering days spent long ago. Shelley swimming, diving, riding and outrunning all of them. Quicksilver, he had called her. She had never been still and had so much energy she sometimes wore him out, even then. He saw her as his future, though he never had the courage to tell her.

And then she had gone away and met David. Better not to dwell on that. Now, he longed to help her, comfort her, but she pushed him away. There had never been anyone else. Several other girls, briefly, but Shelley remained part of him, always overshadowing any relationship he might have had. There was nobody like her.

He looked at the two pups. They had been playing until they were exhausted and were lying in the pen, watching him.

'You could train the pups. If you find her owners they might let you keep them, as a thank-you for rescuing them.' Jamie knelt beside Star, going over her body with his hands. She half lifted her lip at him but then changed her mind, calming down as he spoke to her, his voice soft and reassuring.

'Good lass. You're safe now.' She relaxed. 'I bet the pups inherited her instincts. I'm sure they're pedigrees. She wasn't dumped for having had an illicit liaison. I'd guess she was mated to ensure her offspring could be trained as she has been.'

Star moved, leaning against Greg. Her eyes watched the vet who was now holding the little female. She was tense, ready to jump at him should he harm her baby.

'I'm praying nobody claims her,' Greg said. 'I've never seen a dog like her. Even without her skills she would be a companion for Shelley. I offered to buy her a pup when she came home but it would have been difficult at first. Some months before it was trained and good company. This is entirely different. This one is house-trained, well trained, and so biddable.'

'We'll have to try and find her owner.' Jamie said. 'I'm already corresponding with two of the organizations that train these dogs. One of our clients is disabled and his dog is an enormous benefit. I thought we might find one to help Shelley, but so far there hasn't been one available. I'll ring this afternoon, and see if any has been reported missing. I hope no one does claim her. I think we may have found what we need. I don't suppose we'll be lucky, though. Someone must be missing her badly. '

He turned to go towards the table, and, as he went, he tripped over the edge of the mat. Saving himself with a hand on the back of a chair, he dropped his small appointment diary on the floor. Star was there at once, picking it up and offering it to him.

'My word, she's a star,' he said. 'Just what the doctor ordered.'

Star recognized her name. Her ears pricked, her tail waved, and she almost danced round the room, coming again and again to butt Jamie's thigh and look up at him.

'That could be her name,' he said as he and Greg exchanged amazed glances.

'Star! Come, there's a good lass,' Greg said and she was in front of him in an instant, her tail swishing rapidly, banging against the side of the chair. She had been brought to excited life by hearing that familiar word. The familiar word triggered memories of all she had done before. Her whole body moved in ecstasy.

'Star!' Jamie said. She turned towards him.

'Come.'

She came at once.

Considerably comforted by the discovery of her name, she lay at Greg's feet as he and Jamie drank coffee.

'I must stop this,' Greg said, draining his mug. 'I'll be afloat soon. I seem to have been drinking coffee and tea all morning.'

He went outside with the vet, followed by Meg and Rab. Star lay down beside the pen which held her pups. She belonged here. The past was already fading.

Shelley, exhausted, had gone back to her room intending to sleep till lunch time. She had not slept at all well the night before.

'I can't bear it,' she said as Sheina helped her out of the wheelchair on to the bed. 'Suppose Dannie won't come near me at all? We can't make him, can we?'

'He'll come round.' Like Greg, Sheina was not at all sure that that was true. She sighed as she went back into the kitchen to be met by two men and an excited grandchild spilling over with things to tell her. Dannie couldn't wait to tell her his news.

'Her name's Star. Jamie found out. He said she was a star and she began to dance and get all excited and Grandad says her name must be Star and she can live with us and help Mummy. I can help Grandad with the puppies, and I can have one of them for my own only he won't come and sleep in my room till he's learned to be clean.'

Sheina bent down and hugged her grandson.

'That sounds wonderful. But we've more jobs to do. Going to help us?'

'Yes. Star can come too. Grandad's moving the logs and I can carry little ones and so can Star.'

Greg and Sheina spent the rest of the morning tidying the yard and sweeping away the last of the slush. Dannie helped, carrying small objects and even feeding the hens. Star trotted busily behind them, delighted to be occupied. She too could carry logs. The pups were almost weaned and she was happy to be away from them, though every now and then she checked the kitchen, anxious to make sure all was well.

'Something's happened to him,' Greg said, watching the child run across the yard to the new stack, Star behind him, both carrying small logs. 'I don't know if it was being lost and cold, or it's the dog, or just finding out the truth.'

'Who cares?' Sheina said, feeling as if a huge weight had been lifted from her mind. 'If only it lasts.'

She went indoors to make a quick lunch. Dannie, after considerable persuasion, promised to see his mother as soon as they had all eaten. Shelley was asleep and her mother did not want to wake her. The rest would do her good.

'Working men's rewards,' Greg said, handing out bread

and cheese and tomatoes and pickles. 'You've been a big help today, Dannie. I'm proud of you.'

Dannie had another problem.

'Where do you go when you die? Is my dad is up there?' he asked, pointing out of the window to the now cloudless sky. 'I thought he was still in London. Paul said so. I thought Paul knew everything. He doesn't really, does he? He says people don't go up into the sky anyway.'

'That's not a question anyone can answer,' Greg said. 'A lot of people like to think those they love go there when they die, and we'll all meet again one day, even if that day is a very long way from now.'

'Why does God let people die? If I say my prayers they say God will answer them. He won't send Daddy back, will he? He never answers my prayers, God doesn't.'

Dannie had prayed so hard for his father to come back and fetch him and for Paul to be nice to him all the time, not just sometimes. He thought God never listened. He frowned. He had done a lot of thinking since he read the obituary notice. Suddenly he had to share his fears even though it might land him in worse trouble. Maybe Grandad could help him. Paul didn't tell the truth. But he'd still be there. And what then? Dannie didn't want to go on being known as the naughtiest boy in the school.

'Cowardy. Cowardy. Can't take a dare. Bet you . . .'

The words rang in his ears. Paul said them almost every day.

He couldn't bear it any more.

'I don't want to go back to school. Paul isn't always nice to me. Sometimes he's horrible to me. He takes my money and pulls my hair and hits me with rulers and things and scribbles in my school books and then I get into trouble.'

He put his sandwich down.

'He thinks up things for me to do. Naughty things. Dares. He says I'm a cowardy custard if I don't do them, a sissy boy. And if I don't do them he hurts me. I don't really want to do them but Paul's big and he pinches hard and punches and sometimes kicks me. He hit me with wooden pencil case on the head last week. And he pulls my hair. And takes my money.'

91

Greg felt a surge of anger. So many times in the past, Danny had turned up with a bang or scrape, saying he'd walked into a desk or fallen over. He'd thought Dannie must be unusually clumsy. All those bruises he'd seen on his grandson's small body after he'd brought him in from the barn came painfully to his mind.

'Dannie, those bruises. You didn't get them fighting did you? Or falling down?'

'Paul does them.'

'Why don't you tell your teachers?'

'They wouldn't believe me. I'm the naughty one. Paul never does anything bad. He gets other people to. He hurts them if they don't. He tells us he's better than any of us and he's our king and we have to do as he says. The teachers think he's a very good boy. He's always picked for monitor and they don't know what he's like when they're not there.'

'There are other children he makes do naughty things too?' Greg asked.

'Only two. Liz who's small and rather ugly and Paul says people don't like to look at her, and makes her cry. And Hamish . . . he's small too, and has a funny mark on his face. Paul doesn't make them do things as bad as me. I'm the worst. I'm special . . . he's always telling me that and that's why he thinks up things for me to do.'

Dannie put his plate and mug in the sink. He went outside into the yard. Greg followed him, appalled. Dannie was naughty at times but it sounded as if some of the accusations were unjust, and he was being manipulated by another child for unknown reasons. Why pick on Dannie?

The snow had almost gone. Sheina's tubs of daffodils and crocuses revelled in warm sunshine. Dannie looked at them and then looked up at Greg.

'Can I pick some for Mummy? I haven't been nice to her, have I?'

'I think that your mummy would love them,' Greg said. 'She'll love to have her good boy back again.'

He watched as Dannie picked the flowers, taking great care not to spoil them and intent on making sure that they had long stems.

He took them indoors. He hesitated before opening the

92

door to his mother's room. Shelley was up again, sitting in her wheelchair by the window. She looked out at the hills as she finished her sandwiches.

'I will lift up mine eyes to the hills . . .'

They had always comforted her. They were there before she was born and would be there long after she was gone and all her troubles would be forgotten, melted away in the mists of time. The tops were still white-capped, but it was hard to believe that they had been cut off by snow only the day before.

She turned towards Dannie as he came in. He stood in front of the wheelchair, looking up at her.

'I'm sorry I ran away, Mummy. These are for you.'

He held them out.

She stared at him for a moment, and then leaned forward and hugged him tightly, fighting back tears. Sheina brought in a vase and Shelley arranged them. It was a beginning. The vivid petals brightened the room, bringing with them visions of hope.

'Star,' Dannie said, as an inquisitive face put her nose round the door, anxious to make sure she was not left alone.

The dog came to him and he knelt and put his arms round her.

Star licked his hand.

Jamie, driving home, was worried. Star was exceptional and her training must have taken someone a great deal of time and effort. He was sure she would be claimed. Yet she was ideal for Shelley and might well help her overcome some of her misery.

If the former owners appeared, there would be more unhappiness for Dannie who seemed to have attached himself instantly to the dog. He didn't want that. It was the first sign the child had given of accepting his new environment. Jamie wondered if the aversion to animals had in fact been an act, a protest because the child was so unhappy and had no idea how to counteract that.

Star had value far beyond that of her price as a dog. He turned out of the lane into the main road, wishing life did not throw up so many insoluble problems. He wanted to help

Dannie recover his lost childhood. He wanted Shelley back as she had been when they were teenagers, always full of fun, always laughing. He wondered if she ever laughed now. Her unhappy face haunted him.

There was so little he could do. If only Shelley would let him back into her life. But she had retreated into a shell and none of them could penetrate it. He was sure that the dog would make a tremendous difference.

Maybe he wouldn't telephone and report their find. But he knew he couldn't do that. Someone as disabled as Shelley might well be handicapped now beyond measure, the dog having provided a lifeline. And once you accepted a dog into your heart, its loss was unbearable. No one knew that better than the veterinary surgeons who had administered the last injection. Their surgery would be awash if they collected all the tears that were shed at the final goodbye.

He was sure the dog's owners would be only too anxious to have her home. How had they lost her? He rang after lunch, having put off the dreaded moment.

'Have any of your owners lost a trained dog?' he asked the secretary of the first organization.

'I'll have to ring you back,' she said, and wrote down his number.

There was another organization too. He received the same response.

After more thought, he knew he had to ring the police. Someone might have reported a lost dog.

He waited with dread. Shelley needed the dog, and they could start using her at once if they kept her. Please don't let anyone want her back, he prayed.

His thoughts were not happy. His prayers were rarely answered.

Thirteen

The letter Dannie had brought home was on the mantel-piece in its official envelope. It goaded Greg throughout the weekend. He couldn't make an appointment till Monday. The words burned into his brain:

> We are very concerned about Dannie. It may be necessary to make other arrangements for him, as we cannot have the other children constantly disrupted by his behaviour.
>
> We would like an assessment made by a professional, and then perhaps we may see a way ahead.
>
> It would be useful if we could discuss this and also Dannie's home arrangements. I gather neither parent lives with the child.

And how do you gather that, Madam, Greg thought. What on earth had the child been saying at school? Was he rejecting his mother so completely that he denied her existence? Had he told them his father was actually in London as Paul had made him believe?

He wondered how the Head would react when he told her how Paul had been bullying Dannie. Sheina took the child to the doctor's surgery on the Saturday morning, although he seemed none the worse for his escapade.

'Seems fine,' the doctor said. She frowned at Dannie. 'I hope you won't run away again. You're a very lucky little boy. Suppose your grandad hadn't found you?'

Dannie scuffed his heels against the chair leg. He felt confused. Paul was his friend. Wasn't he? The older boy was so strong and knew everything. He could be kind. There were days when they had fun. Then some demon seemed to possess the other boy, so that he tormented Dannie until he thought he could bear it no longer.

The memory of his terrifying night in the tractor plagued him all weekend, and haunted his dreams, so that Greg spent much of both nights trying to reassure the sobbing child.

Realization hit Dannie for the first time. He shadowed his grandfather, suddenly terrified that he too might suddenly disappear, like his father. He didn't want anyone to go out. They might not come back. Ever.

He dreaded going back to school. Perhaps he could have tummy ache on Monday. Nobody could say he hadn't.

'It might be as well to let him have this week off and keep an eye on him,' the doctor said quietly to Greg afterwards. 'I've seen marks like the ones on his arms before, with children whose siblings are pinching them. Whoever did those was using his nails as well as his fingers. They're really quite nasty. I'd say school's pretty frightening for him at the moment.'

Perhaps, Greg thought, he could clear up the situation at school. Though he had no idea how. 'Could you write me a letter saying that?'

The doctor thought about it. 'I could if you like. I'm not a forensics expert though, so I don't know how much weight it would carry. It certainly wouldn't be iron-clad if it ever came to having to convince a social worker or someone like that.'

'I'd appreciate it if you would,' Greg said. 'I really think we need all the help we can get.'

She had obliged, but still Greg worried endlessly, lying awake at night. There was no doubt whatever that Dannie had been very naughty indeed. The child did not deny it.

Greg could ill afford the time to visit the Head. The village school had closed and Dannie had a ten mile ride each way. Greg or Sheina drove him to the place where the bus stopped to pick up a number of children. Neither of them was happy about the transport and what might go on during the journey, but they couldn't manage a ten mile trip twice every day.

The appointment was at eleven on the Tuesday. Dannie was not going back until Wednesday. If then. Shelley was angry; angry with herself, angry with this unknown child who seemed unusually unpleasant, angry with the school teachers who had not recognized what was happening and been only too willing to blame Dannie. She wanted to find another school, well away from Paul. She did not realize that anger had shocked her out of apathy.

'They seem to be idiots,' she said, after reading the letter. 'How can they think that Dannie's been abandoned by his parents?'

Greg saw a further implication. That the home was not suitable and the child might be taken away from them by intrusive social services people who thought they knew best. The doctor's mention of social workers was chilling: the teachers obviously thought that Dannie's home life was the cause of his bad behaviour. He did not share that idea with either his daughter or his wife, but it nagged at him, no matter what he was doing.

Tuesday came at last. The appointment was at eleven.

He was drinking his second cup of coffee at breakfast when Shelley wheeled herself into the room, dressed for outdoors.

'I'm coming too,' she said. 'It's time I saw the school. I want to see the Headmistress and Dannie's form teacher. I want to know if they know what's going on. I want to tell them what I think of them. They haven't bothered to get to know Dannie at all. I don't want him to go back there. It might be better to teach him at home. That's something I could do, with help from the right people.'

Greg knew that she would be uncomfortable in the Land Rover. The journey would be unpleasant. But Dannie was her son, and it was time she became involved.

He did not know that the thought of the journey terrified his daughter. Last time she had driven anywhere they had crashed. But there was no way she was going to sit at home and worry while her father went alone to the school.

The folding wheelchair had not yet been used. Greg fetched it, and put it into the Land Rover. He lifted her into the passenger seat and helped her to settle comfortably. It was the first time she had shown any desire to venture away from the farm.

The metallic slam of the closing door triggered memory.

97

Shelley clenched her fists. She was trapped, and felt that if she did not take a firm hold on herself, a panic attack would ensue. She breathed deeply, concentrating.

She had to talk, not to think. She racked her brains for a subject. Cars approached them driving fast and she expected every one to hit them.

She had only ridden in the ambulance since the accident as she refused to go out with her parents. They thought she hated being seen in the wheelchair. She did not tell them she was terrified of another crash.

'I wish the village school hadn't closed,' she said as he turned out of the farm lane on to the main road and passed the site that had once housed the place. There was now a row of houses on the old playing fields and the school itself had become offices.

'It was a lovely little place. Everyone knew everyone when I was there. We'd have known Paul and his parents. We'd have known the teachers. Known what went on. Now, it's all so impersonal. That school is far too big. Have you met the Head?'

She was sitting with her fists tightly clenched. She needed to distract herself. Every time she saw an approaching vehicle she clenched her teeth and tried to brake with her feet, but they wouldn't respond. She couldn't even feel them since the accident and sometimes wondered if they were still there.

Memory was a traitor.

She saw the lorry in their way, remembered the appalling crunch as they hit it.

Talk. Anything to distract herself.

'She was away at some county meeting when I called in,' Greg said, resisting the temptation to hoot angrily at a car that overtook too fast on a bend. 'I met her deputy when I went to see the school before Dannie started there.'

And hadn't been impressed, he thought, but didn't say so. She was a small woman, untidily dressed, with an eagerness to talk too much and too fast and an odd way of interspersing conversation with laughter, although nothing amusing had been said.

'I also went to his first parents' evening, last July. I met his form teacher. She asked how Dannie was settling in at home. She didn't mention any school problems.'

Her questions had seemed intrusive, he thought at the time, puzzled by her attitude to him. He felt that she disliked him and couldn't imagine why.

He braked for a Belisha crossing and waited for two women and an elderly man. The little town was busy and there was more traffic than he had expected.

Shelley closed her eyes and swallowed. She wanted to ask her father to turn back, to take her home. The car was a trap, confining her, and she could not move until she was lifted out. Almost as helpless as she had been when . . .

Think of Dannie and the coming interview. She knew she wouldn't like the Headmistress. She intended to tell her exactly what she thought of her and her school. She imagined an elderly martinet with a closed mind. A woman who ought not to be in charge of children.

She dared not look out of the window. Cars and lorries flashed by. Any one of them might hit them. She focused on the pattern of the rug her father had put over her useless legs, hiding them. If she did look out she saw other cars. They all seemed to drive so fast, threatening her. She had to overcome her fear.

The journey ended at last.

High gates opened on to a substantial car park, playing fields beyond it. There were eyes watching through windows of the big modern building when Greg turned the engine off. He opened the wheelchair and lifted Shelley into it, adjusting the rug over her legs.

'I hope there's room for the chair,' Greg said.

Shelley had no intention of being left outside.

'If there isn't she'll have to come out here.'

There was no problem. The doorways were wide and there were no steps. Curious eyes watched them. Shelley wished she had had her automatic chair, but it was too big for the Land Rover. She hated being wheeled like a baby in a pram.

Helen Granger, the Head, was waiting for them in her own room. The secretary led them along a wide corridor, past a cloakroom where the children's clothes hung on hooks, and past several classrooms which had glass windows opening on to the passage. Eyes watched their progress.

Shelley felt as if she would be a curiosity for the rest of her life. A freak, to be stared at as if she were a circus act. Anger helped her. She focused on the forthcoming interview.

Helen Granger was dreading their visit. She had seen Dannie's grandfather at one parents' meeting but hadn't spoken to him. Those nights were so busy and she was always overwhelmed by parents anxious to see her. She remembered a tall man with curly grizzled hair and a very quiet manner.

She had found it difficult to believe the stories that Paul had told her about him. The child had been uneasy, worried about his friend, anxious not to tell tales. Only he felt she ought to know. He had told his form mistress about Dannie's account of his home life and his cruel grandparents. The form teacher felt unable to deal with the situation and had sent the older boy to the Head.

Dannie apparently only confided in Paul, possibly because they were both Londoners and a very small minority among the Scottish children. Paul was such a helpful boy, liked by all the staff. He was always so polite, though he too had had his childhood spoilt by a divorce.

Helen wondered why the boy was so loyal to this young tearaway.

She would have to tell the grandfather that Dannie had to leave. He was too disruptive and she could not have him spoiling lessons for his class mates. Or terrorizing them. She did not know how to tackle the subject of ill treatment that Paul had reported. She suspected that the child needed to be taken away from the elderly couple, who obviously resented him and were too old to cope with such a lively youngster.

She wondered about the mother who stayed away and took no interest in her son. And who had gained a court order to stop the father from ever seeing him, alleging abuse. It seemed Dannie had good reason for his odd behaviour. He had never had a chance, poor child. Really, it was her responsibility to call social services, but she hesitated to do it. This had always been a happy school; she'd never had to deal with an abused child. She didn't feel comfortable setting something so serious in motion without at least trying to meet the family first.

She needed to meet the grandfather, who was apparently

100

coming on his own. His wife had to look after the animals. Helen visualized busy farmers, with no time for a child. Maybe not intentionally unkind, but too old now, and brusque. But those bruises . . . they could no longer be ignored.

She looked in astonishment when Greg came in, pushing a wheelchair in which sat a slight woman with haunted eyes. There had been no mention of a younger woman. Dannie's aunt perhaps?

Greg had not noticed the Headmistress on his previous brief visits to the school. He expected her to be elderly and severe. Shelley expected to dislike her on sight. Both were startled to see a woman no older than Shelley. She was slim, her long hair piled neatly into a chignon. She wore a dark suit with a white blouse ruffled at the neck. A brightly coloured jewelled brooch in the shape of a kingfisher adorned her lapel.

The secretary brought in coffee and chocolate biscuits.

The room was nothing like Shelley had expected. Memories of her own schooldays brought a vision of the bleak office-like room where the Headmaster had dispensed comfort or justice, according to need. He was a kind man who knew all their names and made them laugh.

Here was a rosewood desk, almost hidden away in a recess. Large armchairs were placed round a low oval table on which the secretary put the tray. They could have been in the sitting room of a comfortable house, the curtains, carpet and covers all blending in shades of blue. French doors opened on to a small well stocked garden, surrounded by a wall of warm red bricks. Flowers, skilfully arranged, stood on the windowsill and the top of a low bookcase.

Helen Granger was puzzled by this unexpected situation. She looked at Shelley.

'You are?' she asked.

Shelley stared at her, wondering why she needed to ask.

'I'm Dannie's mother,' she said. 'Hasn't he told you I'm crippled?' It was a word she hated, but she could think of no other explanation. She too was now puzzled. 'Perhaps he hasn't had that much time, as I've only been out of hospital for a couple of months.'

Helen Granger started to wonder if she had to reassess

everything she knew. Now, looking at her unexpected visitor, she saw Dannie's face, although Shelley's was honed by suffering. This woman had the same bone structure, the same arch of the eyebrows, the same sensitive mouth. Only the eyes that looked at her were blue. Dannie's were brown.

Helen sensed resentment, and anger.

She did not know quite how to start the interview.

'I'm sorry, Mrs Barham. No one told me that you lived with Dannie. I understood that you spend your time travelling.' She did not mention the many men who were supposed to take up Shelley's time, to the detriment of her child. 'A child in Dannie's class told me Dannie was an unwanted child, and his grandparents have to care for him as you won't. According to this child, Dannie told him you left his father when he was only a few weeks old, yet in spite of that you prevent the child ever seeing him.'

She didn't mention the beatings. Having only Paul's word to go on, she was disturbed by the appearance of this new factor, and suddenly felt the need to be cautious. She wished she had made enquiries before seeking the interview. Something was very wrong and she felt confused.

Shelley felt a rush of fury. How had this dreadful child come to invent such monstrous lies and, moreover, confide them to the school staff? And worse, how could they have believed him? Dannie couldn't have made up such stories. Her voice, when she did manage to speak, was sharp.

'Mrs Granger, my husband and I were in a very bad car accident just over a year ago. David was killed. I've been in a special hospital as they hoped to get me walking again. They haven't. Dannie had to come to my parents. There was no one else to look after him. My husband's parents are much older than mine. They couldn't possibly have coped with so young a child and are not financially able to employ a nanny.'

She swallowed. It was still difficult to talk about her problems.

'My parents adore him, but he's been very difficult. I only came home a couple of months ago. Dannie seems to have been mesmerized by this boy. It's Paul who told you these things, isn't it? I need to get him away from Paul. If necessary I'll teach him myself. I'm sure I could do it.'

'Paul seems to have a powerful imagination,' Greg said. 'And he's been bullying Dannie terribly. Dannie was too frightened to tell us about it until recently. But he's covered in bruises this boy gave him. I don't know if you will have noticed them, but we have. Dannie was so unhappy that he ran away over the weekend. We had to take him to a doctor yesterday. She told us that he reminded her of other cases of bullying she'd seen. I brought the letter she wrote about it.'

His voice reflected both anger and bewilderment. The lies were so stupid, so pointless, so wicked.

Helen Granger skimmed through the letter Greg handed her. It was brief and to the point: the doctor made no claims of certainty, but testified strongly as to the family's concern for Dannie's welfare, and stated that in her experience, Dannie's scratches and bruises were more consistent with injuries she'd seen inflicted by children than by abusive adults. Mrs Granger stared out of the window at the garden, her thoughts whirling. By all appearances, her visitors were sincere and now as bewildered as she was. The poor mother looked exhausted. She suspected that the grandfather was feeling slightly sick. His puzzled expression and unwinking grey eyes accused her.

'I see I have to adjust my ideas. I thought that explained Dannie's behaviour. I was expecting to find out today that he has a very unhappy home life.'

'I suppose he does,' Greg said. 'Not in the way you think. He was suddenly bereft of his father with his mother unreachable.'

'And now I'm home I can't walk. Dannie refuses to believe that,' Shelley said.

Mrs Granger looked at her, her face thoughtful. She wondered how it felt to suddenly lose the use of your legs.

Greg was trying to voice his own thoughts.

'Dannie's been plunged from a secure and happy home life near London to live with grandparents he has only met very briefly in his short life. He's a very urban child and now he lives on an isolated farm. We don't even have the same accent. It must have been a considerable culture shock. I don't think it has completely dawned on me till now.'

103

Shelley listened. She too had not thought of Dannie's viewpoint. She looked out of the window at the sunny garden. If only life were as peaceful. A blackbird splashed itself in a birdbath. She wanted David beside her, consoling her, telling her this was a bad dream and she would wake up.

The chiming clock returned her to reality.

The Headmistress sighed.

'There's a lot of stress with so many children in the school. It's impossible to know what goes on in their lives. Our ignorance can compound matters. I'll have to look into it, but Dannie isn't the only boy Paul's been telling us things about. If what you're saying is right, we need to be investigating what's going on among the children a lot more. Maybe other children will have stories like Dannie's.'

She stood beside the desk for a moment. She needed time to think. She rearranged two sprays of flowers in the vase. Those bruises. Was Paul tormenting the younger boy and covering up his sins by his cooperation with the adults at school? How many people would believe he could be so devious? How much did she really know about any of her pupils?

'I often wish that this was a small village school.' She resumed her seat opposite Greg. 'With so many children you only really get to know the troublemakers or boys like Paul, who can be so helpful. The other children seem to trust him and confide in him. They tell him family secrets that they wouldn't tell us. Or so I thought,' she added, wondering how many of those tales were also fabricated.

She passed the plate of biscuits to Shelley, who took one to keep her hands occupied.

Greg was thinking about Dannie's confessions.

'He ran away on Friday night, in all that snow. It took me hours to find him. He'd been frightened by an owl and hidden in a tractor and couldn't open the door. The poor little fellow was half dead.'

Sunlight glinted on the silver teapot. A marbled paperweight held down papers on the desk. A pile of exercise books stood on a little table near the door. Greg focused on small details, trying to maintain his temper.

'Dannie told us Paul was going to London with his dad

104

and Dannie could travel with them. Either it was nonsense or the snow prevented them coming. Just as well he didn't come,' Shelley added, suddenly realizing that Dannie might have ended alone in London, gone to their old home, found it had been sold and that he had nowhere to go.

'It was as if a dam burst when Dannie recovered from his adventure,' Greg said. 'He told us things he's never told before. Paul terrorized the child. If Dannie didn't do what Paul wanted, which was always in the form of a dare, the child was bullied mercilessly and his money stolen. He was also hit, with fists, with a ruler, with anything Paul found to hand.'

Shelley was so angry she was shaking. None of this should have happened. Surely the school should have realized what was going on.

'I've never met a boy like Paul,' Mrs Granger said. 'He seems so genuine, a nice boy trying to help an unfortunate companion. All this time we've thought Dannie was the bad influence, with Paul loyally defending his friend, caring about him, and so revealing the reasons for his misbehaviour. It didn't occur to me that the suggestions for mischief might come from Paul.'

The thought of Dannie's suffering angered her. She wondered how she was going to deal with Paul.

'He seems to have a very devoted father,' Greg said. 'I think Dannie was jealous of the fact that the boy has all these exciting weekends and he had nothing.'

'Exciting weekends?' Mrs Granger asked.

'Yes, Dannie says that Paul's father took him all sorts of places, landing fields for aeroplanes and expensive restaurants. Dannie and his father used to do things together all the time. He must have envied Paul his father.'

'Paul's mother left his father when Paul was four years old,' Mrs Granger said. 'He was an alcoholic and both she and the boy suffered. There was a very unpleasant court case after he beat her and injured the child. He received a jail sentence. She moved away and changed her name. I believe when he came out he emigrated and moved in with another woman. Those wonderful outings are complete fiction. This is the first I've heard of them. The mother's a dental receptionist, working hard to keep them both.'

'Can you do anything at all to keep the boys apart?' Greg asked.

'I must, though I need to think about it. In the short term I'll move Paul to a different class. I can think up some reason.'

'You can't keep them separate at break and dinner time,' Shelley said.

'I'll find a way. Don't worry. This must be sorted.'

'You will give Dannie time to settle?' Shelley asked. 'He's had enough upset in the past year, without being sent away to a special school.'

'I'll make certain that nothing like this happens again,' Mrs Granger assured her.

She watched as Greg wheeled Shelley out of the room. Dannie's form mistress had said that she felt something was going on that she didn't understand. She had had reservations about Paul, which none of the rest of the staff shared. Maybe he was born to act, Mrs Granger thought. She would need to bear that in mind when she spoke to him.

Shelley kept her mind on the interview all the way home. If she didn't think about the car she could manage the journey without revealing her fears to her father. She was unaware that Greg had noticed the clenched fists, and the deep breaths she took whenever anything approached them.

They were both thankful to reach home. Dannie was playing with the dogs, which was a new development, and pleased both of them. Rab's paw was almost healed. Meg tired of the game and lay down and watched them.

Star left the game and came to greet Greg and Shelley.

Maybe life would improve, Shelley thought. Now they had to tell Dannie of his friend's perfidy.

Dannie listened quietly when his grandfather told him that Paul had invented his various weekend activities and that his father had left the family and gone to live abroad with somebody else. Star lay beside him, as if trying to impose her calmness on him. She was so gentle and persistent in her attempts to woo him that she had removed his worry about the dogs.

'Why did Paul make all that up?' Dannie asked.

'I'd think that he wishes they were true, and wants his

father as badly as you want yours,' Greg said. 'He's a very sad little boy, Dannie. Also a very mischievous one. I think you should keep away from him.'

Which they both knew might not be at all easy.

That night Greg went into his grandson's room at bedtime to read him a story.

'Can Mummy read to me tonight?' he asked.

It was the first time he had asked for her. Shelley wished she could climb into his bed and hold him tightly but many movements hurt too much to risk that.

She sat for a long time after Dannie had fallen asleep, looking down at him, hoping desperately that this was the start of a new rapport between them. She stroked his cheek before turning her chair to go out. He woke and smiled up at her.

'I did this for you,' he said, and brought a piece of paper out from under his pillow.

It was a list of everything that Star had done so far. Dannie still found writing difficult. It had taken him a long time. Maybe now his schoolwork would improve.

Shelley bent to hug him and to kiss him.

'Grandad says I can have Star's puppies and we'll teach them everything Star knows,' he said.

Star. She was a hope and a promise. If only nobody claimed her.

Dannie smiled sleepily at his mother.

'There was a new moon,' he said. 'I wished.'

Fourteen

Shelley wondered what her son had wished. She would wish that she could walk again. Maybe the doctors were wrong.

She had to try for Dannie's sake. David was gone. Her son depended on his mother. She had to make an enormous effort to face the world in her wheelchair. She had refused all offers of outings, thinking that as she had only been home for a couple of months, she needed time to adjust.

It was not till the visit to the school that she realized she had a major problem. She had half suspected it, but now she had to face the truth. She had not expected that when the car door shut on her, panic would overwhelm her. They were going to crash. Every approaching vehicle was a threat. She wanted her father to take her back to safety. She never wanted to travel by car again.

She did not share her fears with anyone else. They seemed absurd when spoken aloud. Perhaps if she had been able to ride in a car only a few days after the accident she would have overcome her terror by now. But it was over a year ago. It had not been quite so bad lying in the ambulance which brought her home. She couldn't see out of the windows and she had slept for much of the way.

Dannie, now that Paul was no longer dictating to him, discovered that dogs were fun. Greg told him the two pups were his, as nobody had claimed their mother. Dannie was to feed them and play with them, and Greg would show him how to teach them.

He had to be very responsible and grown up, but Greg trusted him to look after them well. He named them Amber and Hero.

He had been away from school for three days when the

Headmistress telephoned to say she had had a long session with Paul's mother, who decided the best thing they could do was move him to another school, one that specialized in handling emotional problems. She had been unaware of the tales he'd told Dannie and was horrified.

Greg wondered how his mother would cope. Paul had far more problems than Dannie.

Dannie felt as if his world had been overturned. The dread he felt each day when preparing for school was gone. He no longer had to be naughty to please Paul. Perhaps all his wishes would come true. He had wished that Paul would go away. And Paul had gone. Nobody else had ever bullied him. Nobody bullied him now.

No use wishing for his father to come back. That he now knew was impossible. He was very quiet both at school and at home. Nobody yet realized he had not grieved for David before because he was sure his father was really still alive. All his energy had been spent in hating his mother because he knew she had sent his father away.

'He seems to have grown up overnight,' Sheina said, after Shelley and Dannie had gone to bed. She was even more worried about the child. 'I almost wish he'd be naughty. This is too good to last.'

'We should have realized something was going on,' Greg said. 'I just thought he was an exceptionally difficult child and his parents had spoiled him.'

Dannie recognized that nothing could ever be the same again. Greg explained that his old home now belonged to somebody else. He took Dannie with him when they went to see the minister about a memorial plaque in the church. A place to visit, to bring flowers, to remember. With it came the knowledge that neither of his parents had betrayed him.

Afterwards they went into town and bought a wooden seat to put in the little public garden next to the graveyard. Dannie chose the words and the lettering. It read 'Dedicated to the memory of David John Barham.'

A week later Sheina planted a rose bush in the flower bed beside it.

'Daddy doesn't seem so far away now,' Dannie said when his grandmother took him to see it. He looked up at the sky.

'I hope he isn't lonely without us in Heaven. Do you think he can see us?'

Sheina was startled and it was a moment before she thought of a reply.

'I don't think Heaven's a lonely place. I'm sure he's watching over us,' she said.

Dannie traced the letters of the plaque with his fingers.

Nobody claimed Star. Each day they felt more sure that she was now theirs. Each day the dog endeared herself further with her own actions. Each day Shelley came to rely on her more.

Star discovered that her new home presented her with the challenges she needed. She watched all the humans who came into her life. She saw that Shelley could not pick up anything that fell on the floor. Picking up had been a game she had played daily in her old home.

She shadowed the wheelchair, ready at once to take action. As the days went by her memories of the past grew dim. She played with Dannie. Greg devised a series of games for them both. Dannie hid things for Star to find. Star found new things to do. She pulled off Shelley's socks and trousers for her. She carried slippers and shoes to their owners.

The dog learned new words and knew the names of many household objects. She brought Greg his car keys. She helped Sheina find the eggs each morning. Star could pick them up without breaking them, and put them gently in the basket.

'She's a godsend,' Sheina said one morning at breakfast. 'She saves my back. And she can find the eggs of any hen who has decided to go off and brood them away from the nest boxes.'

Greg had been dubious at first about allowing Star to wander freely on their territory. However, she made no attempt to chase poultry or any other farm stock. The barn cats soon learned that they were safe with her, though not with the pups, who had to be taught that dogs don't chase cats, whatever they think about them.

Star had discovered, in her earlier life, that she could make people laugh. It was a sound she loved and she spent much of her time devising new ways of amusing her human companions.

Dannie, early one morning, on his way to join his grandfather for his journey to the school bus stop, was diverted by the sight of the Golden Retriever dragging the largest wellington he had ever seen across the yard. She had found it in the barn. Greg, coming to see where Dannie had gone, as they were likely to be late, saw Star, and joined in the laughter.

'It's a giant's wellie,' Dannie said, as he looked at it in disbelief and wondered if maybe the giant was still around, maybe hiding in the barn, which he still disliked, even though he now knew that the ghost had really been the owl. Greg had a sudden memory that made him smile.

'It belonged to one of the men who used to work here,' he said. 'Alastair was very tall, around six foot eight. Maybe he *was* a giant. He was always joking and one day he said he had brought your Gran a present.'

'What was it?'

'A wellie planted with marigolds. Your Gran didn't like it much but kept it outside the door till Alastair left. The wellie has a hole in it. She must have dumped it in the barn. Come on, or we'll miss the school bus.'

'Star's extra specially clever, isn't she?' Dannie asked, as Greg turned out on to the main road.

'Very definitely,' Greg said. He was still worried by the thought that someone was missing her. Someone, he suspected, who needed her skills and for whom she had been trained. There was nothing he could do about that.

As the days passed they realized that she was indeed a boon. She lifted Shelley out of the pit of depression. The dog knew just what absurd antic would make her new owner laugh. She was always ready to invent new ways of having fun.

Dannie had given his mother a teddy bear and a toy rabbit for her birthday. Sheina, once she had made Shelley's bed, always sat them against the pillows. Star invented a new game that became a frequent occurrence whenever Shelley felt life had become more than she could endure.

Star recognized when her mistress was unusually unhappy and stood in front of her, bending her front legs, enticing her to join in the fun. If Shelley ignored her, she barked. It was a game she never shared if anyone else was in the room.

'You wouldn't . . .' Shelley said, when she saw this, knowing what was to come.

'It's ridiculous,' she said one evening, while they were eating their evening meal. 'It's just as if she says, plain as plain, "Oh, yes, I would."'

Star's eyes were alight with mischief. She jumped on to the bed, seized either Teddy or Bun and jumped off, racing round the room, throwing whichever trophy she held into the air and catching it again.

Shelley only had to say 'enough', and the game ended with her holding the toy on her lap. Star might be intent on her work, but she never lost her sense of fun. The pups inherited it and the three dogs brought laughter back into their lives.

In the early days Dannie had been uncertain, but Star wooed and won him, so that his first thought when he came from school was to find her. His fear of the dogs vanished. Without Paul to mock him whenever he spoke of the farm, he was beginning to be interested in the other animals.

Greg gave him two of the orphan lambs. He bottle-fed them and watched over them when they joined the other ewes. Their lambs would be his, Dannie was told. One day he would have his own flock. One day he would inherit the farm.

'Would you like that, Dannie?' his grandfather asked.

'All of it?' he asked, incredulous. All those fields and animals and the house and barns . . . all his.

'All of it,' Greg assured him.

'I think perhaps I would.'

The farmhouse, built when Queen Victoria was still a baby, had once housed a huge family of children as well as several servants. There were eight bedrooms, which included three large attics. The servants' quarters were separated from the house by a green baize door. Beyond it had been the old kitchen, a sitting room, and a bathroom.

This was ideal for Shelley and her son. After conversion their rooms connected and Star positioned herself midway between them. If Dannie woke in the night, plagued by dreams of ghosts, she padded into him and nosed him. She curled up by his bed, but in the morning she was always back at her post, watching for Shelley's needs.

Dannie now came daily into his mother's room to dress. Star brought him his shoes and socks.

'She looks so proud,' he said one morning.

Shelley, who enjoyed watching the performance, smiled.

'She has every right to feel proud.'

She was beginning to appreciate the benefits the dog had brought with her. Before Star's arrival, Shelley felt trapped. If she dropped her book, or her pen, she couldn't always reach to pick it up, even with the grab stick her father had bought her. It was very useful but she hated it. It was a symbol of her helplessness.

She had to wait for someone to be free to come and help her. Now she had no need. Star was ready to spring up at once and pick up anything that had fallen. She was a companion when everyone else was busy. She brought a new freedom from the imprisonment of the chair, and a feeling of independence that had been lacking when Shelley first came home.

Both Jamie and Angus called frequently, fascinated by the dog's numerous and increasing skills. Star learned to hold a bottle for an orphan lamb. She could bring Shelley her purse, or the phone, or the book she was reading, apparently knowing the words for each.

She gave Shelley a confidence that she had been lacking, so that now on fine days she was happy to wheel herself outside, watch the dogs play, and greet anyone who came to the farm. She took over all the cooking, and then began to serve in the farm shop. This shop was set up in a converted barn, to which had been added a large greenhouse, where Sheina grew organic salad ingredients. Greg had designed it so that the aisles were wide enough for Shelley's chair, and everything was grown at waist height in specially constructed beds on top of benches designed especially to give her easy access. When she was serving behind the counter, nobody could see the chair, or realize she was disabled.

Car journeys were still a problem, and dreams of the crash plagued her almost nightly. She slept badly as a result, and was only too ready to join Sheina when she got up at five.

There was time to make cakes which sold out every day, and she added little pies and quiches, which were soon in big demand for children's lunches and a quick and easy meal at home. Once she was busy the days passed fast with little time for thought.

The nights were bad. Too much time lying awake. Coming back to her childhood home had awakened long-forgotten memories. She remembered the days when she got up early to groom her pony, ready for the day's outing and the competitions.

She and Jamie had both been only children, Jamie the older by seven months. They became closer than many a brother and sister. They were always vying for first place in the showjumping competitions. There was time then for her parents to take her. The horse box was still in the barn. She wondered why her father hadn't sold it. But maybe he hoped that Dannie would want to ride.

There were nights when she dreamed she was running again. She was riding again. The horse soared over the jumps. She was no longer competing against Jamie, but against David. She remembered the dreams and could not imagine why her husband appeared in them, as David couldn't ride and had never had any desire to try. What he wanted was a racing car. In those dreams he swung her from the saddle and held her close, kissing her. The dreams always ended and she came to back to reality, and a pillow wet with tears.

She woke to the knowledge that David would never hold her again and that she was trapped for ever in a body that refused to obey her. Sleep, after such dreams, was impossible. Greg bought her an automatic bed that lifted her into a sitting position. She switched on the light, and reached for her book. Star, when the light came on, always jumped to the seat of the chair beside her mistress and lay with her nose over Shelley's arm, her whole body offering comfort.

When morning came at last, Shelley supervised the dogs' first outing, knowing that if the pups misbehaved, Star would round them up and take them indoors. Star had house-trained them, taking them out when necessary. The ritual was always the same. Meg and Rab and the pups greeted Star, and then the younger dogs raced off to play wildly round the yard, full of life and energy.

Meg tired easily and spent less time on the hills. Star needed to watch Shelley, and her game ended soon, as she came back to sit where she could see anything that was needed.

'I envy the dogs,' Shelley said in an unguarded moment to Jamie, who had called in on his way from another farm. He often stayed for meals when they were children and now he slipped back into his old ways as if there had been no break.

This time he had called in early to take Dannie to school.

'Save Greg a journey,' he said. 'I was at McLeans' till breakfast time. Their Shire has a lovely filly foal. As I had to pass . . .'

'Bacon and eggs?' Shelley asked.

'They fed me. Royally. I won't need to eat again today.'

He grinned at Dannie who was finishing his own breakfast. Jamie walked beside Shelley as she propelled her chair into the yard. The sun flooded the distant hills, dappling them with light.

'You're getting stronger daily,' Jamie said. 'You never know. Next year you may be running with the pups.'

'And Toffee will have kittens,' Shelley said.

Dannie, who had joined them, ready for his journey to school, looked up at her.

'Cows don't have kittens, Mummy,' he said. 'They have calves. Jamie says Toffee will have a new calf next month.'

He looked at his mother and the vet in bewilderment when they laughed.

'Your mum was being daft, Dannie,' Jamie said. 'Of course Toffee won't have kittens.' He paused. 'I used to help my Dad when the calves were born. Would you like to help me?'

Dannie was not sure about that.

'Tell you what,' Jamie said. 'If it's a nice day next Saturday suppose we all go fishing? Your mum can sit and watch us and I'll show you how to catch trout. There's a good place with the road very near. You can borrow my dad's fishing rod. We can have a picnic.'

'Can we?' Dannie asked. 'Can Star and the pups come?'

'Star can come, but not the pups. They're too naughty. They need a lot more training. We'd have to tie them up and that's no fun for them.' Jamie said. He looked anxiously at Shelley. 'How about it? A change of scene will do you good.'

'Suppose the chair bogs down in the field?' Shelley refused to acknowledge that that was not what was worrying her. She still hated any car journey and avoided them whenever possible. Jamie's car was even smaller than Greg's Land Rover.

'I can carry you from the car to the chair,' Jamie said.

'I'm too heavy,' Shelley said. She hated the ignominy of being lifted like a small child.

'I carry calves and sheep and they're a sight more unco-operative. I take it you won't kick me and try to bite?'

In spite of herself Shelley joined Dannie in his laughter.

'Please, Mummy,' he said, his eyes begging her. David's eyes, always inviting her to join in some crazy exploit. 'Come on Shelley, it'll be fun' . . . the memory hurt.

It would be a treat for Dannie. Man things, David used to call them on the days when he and his son took off to watch a football match or go on some excursion from which she was excluded. Greg never had time for that.

'Why don't you and Dannie go by yourselves? I'll be a nuisance.'

'We want you,' Jamie said.

He wanted Shelley to go out and about, and he would make sure she did, even if he had to drag her there. Much better if she came willingly.

'Please, Mummy, please.' Dannie was almost dancing with impatience.

'It'll do you good,' Sheina said, having come into the yard in time to hear Jamie's proposition.

Maybe it'll rain and then we can't go, Shelley thought, even as she agreed.

She had hoped that with time the panicky feelings would die away, but instead they seemed to grow worse with each journey, however short. Her throat closed, her fists clenched and she was overcome with fear. She couldn't confess. It was so stupid.

The night before their trip, she dreamed. She was looking

116

for David. He had gone out without her, and she suddenly found herself alone. She was back in their London home, and, frantic with worry, she set out to look for him. She did not have time to dress. Wearing pyjamas and slippers, she ran out into the cold night. She turned into a narrow street, tall houses overshadowing her. There was a roar as a huge lorry came speeding towards her, growing ever bigger, until it engulfed her.

She screamed.

She woke as Star's cold nose pushed against her neck. The light went on and Dannie stood there, staring at her, his eyes wide and frightened.

'I'm sorry, darling. It was a bad dream,' she said.

Her bedside clock read two a.m.

She could hear her mother's steps on the stairs.

'Only a dream,' she said again.

'Mummy will be all right now,' Sheina said. 'You never dream the same dreams twice.'

She led Dannie back to bed and tucked him in and kissed him.

'I didn't know grownups had bad dreams,' he said. 'I thought it was only children. Mummy said I'd grow out of them.'

'Everyone has bad dreams sometimes. Only Mummy's won't be like yours,' she said.

She switched off the light and went back to her daughter.

'I'm sorry,' Shelley said. 'I didn't mean to wake anyone. I must have screamed aloud. Star woke me.'

Star had settled on the chair, her nose on the edge of Shelley's bed.

'What were you dreaming?'

She could still see the lorry. Not that in her dream, but the one that had hit them. The memory recurred almost every day. The weeks after the accident were still blurred but the moment of the crash remained vivid.

'I've forgotten,' she said.

She did not want to sleep again. She adjusted her bed, switched the light back on again and read, but the story did not grip her. She could never go with Jamie and Dannie tomorrow. The mere thought of the journey made her sweat.

Jamie arrived at ten. He had borrowed his father's car, which was much larger than his, and he and Greg installed Shelley on the back seat, the dog beside her. She couldn't refuse to go. Dannie was dancing with excitement and Jamie was obviously delighted at the thought of their expedition. She clenched her fists and shut her eyes. If she couldn't see . . . but the panic remained, almost choking her. She prayed that Jamie wouldn't notice. It was so feeble. She had never known such fear in her life.

At last they arrived. The meadow beside the lake was bathed in sunshine. Beyond, the mountains reached to the sky, untroubled by clouds. The farmer who owned the land met them and helped Jamie carry Shelley to a level place where he had put her chair. She sat between them on their crossed hands. She felt like a baby, and hated her helplessness even more, but everyone seemed determined that she should enjoy the day.

'Be back at teatime,' the farmer said, 'or if it rains.' He smiled at Dannie. 'Good luck.'

Shelley suddenly realized that this was not the smaller wheelchair but a comfortable garden chair that Jamie had borrowed from his own home. For a while she could pretend she was normal again, and independent, just sitting like anyone else, enjoying the view. She would get up and walk to the car. If only . . .

The early autumn sun was warm. The massed trees on the far bank glowed with colour. Behind them the mountains bulked on the horizon, dappled by light that shifted constantly as the wind blew scattered clouds across the sun. A bird, perched on a branch of a nearby tree, sang joyously.

For the first time since the accident, Shelley felt at peace. She was content to sit and watch, to listen to the wind murmuring in the branches, to the tiny slap of small waves that shivered against the shore. Jamie was showing Dannie how to use his rod. His mother had unearthed one that Jamie himself had had when a boy. The dark head bent close to the blonde child, explaining carefully. David would never have been so patient, Shelley thought, and then guilt needled her. David had always done his best.

Other thoughts crept in, unbidden. They had always done

118

what David wanted, never what they wanted. They had been swept along by his energy and his enthusiasm. He never asked if I was tired, Shelley thought. Even the day before Dannie was born, we went out for a meal. He could never stay at home. All I wanted was sleep.

Dannie cast his fly into the water. Jamie watched and then turned to grin at Shelley, his thumb up.

'Well done,' he said.

David would never have praised the child so easily, though he would have chided him if he had been slow. Shelley felt disloyal, comparing the two men.

Jamie cast and took up his position on the bank.

'Don't talk or you won't catch anything,' he said. 'Fish have very good hearing. The slightest sound and they vanish. They can see you too, so pretend to be a tree.'

Dannie grinned.

Her son had changed so much in the past months, Shelley thought. A year and a half had flown by since the accident. Star lay quiet, on guard, ever watchful lest she was needed. She must be three or four years old. Shelley had never in her life loved any dog like this. Star was her constant companion, her lifeline, her sanity. She reached her hand out and the golden head lifted, eyes loving, waiting to be petted.

A gentle wind rippled the sleek water. Shelley suddenly realized that this was what she had missed, all those years in London. The lake and the hills and the wide expanse of moorland soothed her, removing pain and guilt.

For the first time for years she felt free, the quiet seeping through her, so that she was entirely relaxed.

She forgot her useless legs. She had weathered the journey in spite of her conviction that they would crash. Jamie drove carefully, unlike David who was ruthless in overtaking and cutting in. He approached junctions at speed, slamming on the brakes at the last minute.

One day, an accident was inevitable, she thought. David was always in a hurry, always wanting results yesterday. They sped through the days without time to relax or think.

Better to forget that. She glanced at her watch and called. 'Lunch time.'

Jamie's mother had prepared a feast of cold guinea fowl with green salad and coleslaw, all in individual containers. There was lemon meringue pie to follow. Dannie had a fairy cake, iced, with his name on it in chocolate whirls.

'Your mum always does make great meals,' Shelley said. 'I'd forgotten. I would never have gone on picnics as a child if your parents hadn't insisted I came too.'

'You and Jamie?' Dannie asked. 'When you were both as old as me?'

'We started school the same day,' Jamie said. 'Your mum's birthday's in August and mine's January, so we were both six in the same year. I was one of the oldest in the class and she was one of the youngest.'

'Was Mummy naughty ever?'

'We were all naughty sometimes,' Jamie said. 'Nobody's good all the time.'

'What did you do?'

Jamie decided their pranks were best forgotten in case they gave Dannie ideas. They tidied up the picnic things to distract him.

Dannie fished, promising to stay where they could see him and not to go too near the edge of the bank. Jamie stretched out on the grass by Shelley's chair, lying on his back, his hands behind his head. Star positioned herself half between Shelley and her son, ready for action if needed.

A little brown duck swam past, a file of tiny ducklings behind her. A heron flew over and landed further down the bank, standing, immobile, watching the water. His beak speared down in a sudden flash of movement as he caught a tiny fish. Leaves whispered in a small wind that turned the grey blue waters of the lake into ruffled silk.

'Glad you came?' Jamie asked.

'It's so peaceful. And Dannie's loving it.'

'Poor little guy. He's had a rough time,' Jamie said. 'Made worse by misunderstandings and his fear of Paul. Fear's the very devil.'

Shelley wondered if he had noticed how tense she was during the drive.

'I was afraid of riding,' he said. 'When we started. Do you remember? You were five and I was just six. We had

120

almost identical ponies. Heron, the lovely little cob your dad bought after Bracken died, and my Rocket. I loved Rocket but I didn't want to ride him. Dad said, "Don't be silly. Shelley can ride. Of course you can too." But I was so scared I felt sick.'

Shelley turned her head to stare down at him.

'You? How could you be? Look at the times you beat me.'

'I did overcome it, up to a point. It was the only way I could be with you,' Jamie said. 'I never quite grew out of it. You soared over the biggest jumps . . . my pony often refused but that was because I funked them, and he knew it.'

There were small white clouds building over the distant hills. The tops were shrouded. Jamie had never confessed his fears before. People are like the hills, he thought. So much of them is hidden in the clouds they generate to hide their real feelings.

'I think there are two kinds of people,' he said. 'Watchers and doers. Every week there are those who go out and play games, while thousands more just watch them. I'd have been happier to watch, only Dad insisted I rode. And I wanted your admiration.'

And his father's too, he thought. Dad was always holding Shelley up as an example. She was much braver than he, always ready for a challenge, and here was Angus lumbered with a son who thought three times before doing anything.

Jamie sighed.

'Did you get over your fear?'

'Yes, mostly. Not when we had big jump-offs. I never beat you then. You were always ahead. Whatever you did, I was usually second. You seemed to be afraid of nothing and I always had to nerve myself to follow.'

He laughed, but it was not a happy sound.

'The desire of the moth for the flame. I think most of the sixth form had a crush on you. But I never grew out of mine.'

Shelley watched a bird dip towards the water, and then fly up. A dragonfly shimmered just beyond her chair. The sun glittered on its iridescent body and papery wings. Dannie was absorbed, watching his float, praying for a bite.

'You always had other girls,' Shelley said.

'I was trying to cure myself of you. I knew you weren't interested. We were friends . . . maybe I was your brother. But that wasn't what I wanted. Then you went away . . . and David came into your life.'

David. She still ached for him. He had been so alive, making the most of every minute. Life with him was never easy, as some of his ideas were wild. They had gone on a boating holiday with a three-month-old baby. Their friends thought he was mad, and so did she, but he persuaded her. Nothing could go wrong. Most of the time she had been worried sick, especially when the engine failed in a storm. David just laughed. Lightning flashed and thunder roared as he worked. The waves seemed mountainous. She was sure it never would start again and he had neglected to make sure they had radio contact with the shore.

'There, you see,' he said in triumph when once more they were under way. Dannie had slept most of the time, and seemed untroubled by the boat's movement.

'It could have been worse,' she said to those who asked, not confessing she had lived in a permanent nightmare, afraid they might sink, they would all drown. Motherhood had changed her. She was responsible for this small life. Fatherhood had not tamed David.

'David . . .' It was still hard to talk about him. 'He was exciting,' she said.

'And I was just boring old Jamie, always predictable.'

Only then did Shelley realize that Jamie had always been there for her, a rock to lean on, till she went away from home to university. She never came back for more than short visits. In the old days she could always ask his advice. David never had any to give.

'Oh, forget that. Let's . . .' he'd say. And off they went on some new adventure, with Shelley ever more reluctant to take risks. David never saw danger. He ran headlong into all kinds of self-induced problems but nearly always managed to survive them. Till that last time, when he killed himself.

And condemned me to this, she thought, achingly aware of her useless legs again.

'David was so full of energy,' Shelley said. 'We went on a holiday in Canada three weeks before Dannie was due. I don't know why he wasn't born on the plane. I went into labour almost as soon as we got home. I was so tired, but David never stopped. He was perpetual motion in human form. Must see the sights now we're here. May never get the chance again. Come on, Shelley, it's not that far.'

Star put her head on Shelley's knee, sensing her feelings. She stroked the dog. A warm tongue licked her hand.

'All the same, I loved David. And we were very happy,' she said. A niggling feeling asked if that were true, but she pushed it away.

Jamie sat up and stared at the water. A small wind danced the waves and frothed the tops with white. Dannie turned his head and smiled at them. Memory betrayed her. The vivid expression was David all over again. She looked away, memories flooding. A moment later the float dipped, and Jamie went to help him land a tiny trout.

'Too small,' Jamie said, as he carefully unwound the hook from its mouth. Dannie took it and put it into the water, watching it swim away.

Shelley was glad that Jamie was not beside her. A wave of misery overwhelmed her and at once Star's urgent nose pressed into her hand returning her to the present, but the peace was shattered. She needed to be alone. Dannie would remind her, more and more, of David. Would that ever stop hurting?

The sun, echoing her mood, vanished behind a bank of clouds, threatening rain. The cool wind strengthened, punishing trees that rocked and cried as it sped through them. The long grass on the other side of the ruffled water dipped and rose in waves. Star shook herself, objecting to the unseen fingers that lifted her fur.

Shelley was cold. She wanted to get up and walk back to the car. She did not want to sit here. She was not going to call out for help.

'I'm so useless,' she said, as Jamie came back to her. He took off his jacket and put it round her shoulders. 'Why won't my legs work?'

'You aren't useless at all. Your parents were almost giving up when you had your accident. You've inspired them with fresh energy. The foot and mouth epidemic crippled the farm.'

'But they didn't get it.'

'There would have been compensation if they had. As it was, they couldn't sell the sheep or the wool or the lambs . . . and no money was coming in. They were too tired to think of other ways of making an income. In six months you've got them trying new ventures like the farm shop. You've expanded that and taken over most of Sheina's work, and freed her to help Greg. You've made an enormous difference.'

The threatened rain began, driving into their faces on the rising wind.

The farmer who had given them permission to fish in his river came back.

'Time to go,' he said. 'This is going to get worse.'

Dannie and Jamie packed their rods.

They reached the car just as the storm began. Star followed them, watchful, as if sure she needed to guard them all from danger. She jumped in beside Shelley. Jamie ran back for the picnic basket and her chair, his head soon white with hail.

'You should have waited till it stopped,' Shelley said, when he returned. Laughing, he rubbed his hair with a towel.

'You're cold. I should have noticed the change in the weather. I want you home and warm again.'

He switched on the car heater.

Shelley thought over their conversation as they drove home. She had never realized that Jamie was afraid of jumping. He hid it well. Was David afraid of showing fear, always forcing himself to face yet another challenge and show a brave face to the world?

She wished she understood people better. As it was, they often baffled her. It was not until she was back in her own room that she realized she had not once worried about crashing.

Life settled into a new routine. Shelley still hated her wheelchair, but now the fear of driving had receded, and was only a faint background worry, triggered by someone else's folly. Both her father and Jamie were thoughtful drivers. She only consented to visit isolated places. She hated the pity in strangers' eyes, or the quick glance and the turned head, as they realized they did not know how to react to her.

Dannie wrote about Star at school, with the result that the farm soon had a number of children visiting to watch her perform for them. Star enjoyed an audience.

'The children love coming,' Shelley said one morning, while they were drinking coffee. 'We could do teas . . . do you remember the cream teas we used to do when I was growing up? I always wondered why you stopped them.'

'No time.' Sheina looked at the yard. Grass grew between the cobbles. The whole place needed to be smartened. 'We had help on the farm then.'

'It needn't be in a big way,' Shelley said. 'I can make cakes and scones; and we can give them a boiled egg, home-made bread and farm butter. There won't be many at first. They can eat in the kitchen. Summer holidays are starting, and the children are good for Dannie. He has friends now.'

'What do you think?' Sheina asked Greg that night after Shelley and Dannie had gone to bed. 'It will be a lot of work. We can't just start it and then stop it. People will come expecting tea, and find we don't do it any more. And then they might stop coming to the farm shop.'

'We might expand that even more,' Greg said. 'Shelley's coming out of her shell. I'm sure Maggy would come in and help.'

Maggy Brook had offered to come any time some years before, when her husband died tragically as the result of a tractor accident. She missed their own farm, and saw an opportunity to stay in the village and help her neighbours at the same time. She had left when Shelley came home, as Sheina thought it would be necessary to close the shop. She had expected her daughter to be almost helpless and take up all her spare time.

The shop was popular as everything was locally grown and fresh. They sold home-produced meat, home-cured bacon, and their own eggs. Neighbours brought their surplus fresh vegetables and in season there was always fruit. The minister's wife provided a constant supply of jams and chut-neys. Shelley already made cakes and bread and biscuits, which had a ready market. Forced to sit all day she had to find occupation, and began to embroider again. Her cushion covers were soon in demand with orders coming in.

She found that being busy kept misery at bay. The more she had to do, the more likely she was to sleep through the night and the dreams were less frequent, though she still dreamed of running and swimming.

'Shelley thinks we ought to do bed and breakfast as well,' Sheina said one morning at coffee time. Greg was working on the yard, pulling up the grass. Maggy was painting the fence. Sheina had bought big tubs to brighten the place, and they were now full of flowering plants. They were all glad of a break.

'A lot of extra work,' Greg said.

'I can cook the breakfasts, Dad. And Star helps with the washing. It just leaves Mum to strip the beds and make them again and change the towels. It would help the farm income no end.'

'Be easier to turn the top field into a camping and caravan site,' Greg said.

'And then we have to make provisions for showers and toilets, and there will be children running around. Litter and gates left open and we have their rubbish to dispose of as well. Bed and breakfast is much simpler.'

Shelley had been thinking about it during her wakeful nights. It was better than fretting about all she couldn't do. She needed, desperately, to have a purpose. If she could contribute in a major way to the farm income, she would be happier to accept that life was never going to change and she would never walk again.

'We can try it,' Greg said. 'If it overloads you all, then we stop.'

Shelley contacted the tourist board. Greg bought a computer for the business and Jamie set up a website for her. Soon bookings were coming in. Farm holidays were popular.

One day Jamie brought a Star a thick length of knotted multi-coloured rope. That was familiar and woke memories of Liz. They had played tug of war so often. She hauled on the rope happily, and he left it with her when she pulled it away. She took it to Shelley, who began to play the game too. It would strengthen her arms.

Star never wanted to let go. She pulled hard, and when

126

Shelley managed to get the rope from her, she became even more determined. The game was not progressing as it should. It became an ongoing tournament, Star versus Shelley, with possession of the rope always in dispute. Then, six weeks later, Shelley, hanging on, laughing at the dog's efforts, was pulled out of her chair.

Disbelieving, she stood, and counted to four before she fell back.

Shelley wanted to yell with joy, but this had to be kept secret. Too soon, yet. She might never go further. But if . . . Her life was made up of 'ifs'.

She had stood, alone. No one but Star helping her. She had not fallen. Next time she would stand for longer. She would move her feet. She had a new goal. A future.

Star released her hold.

Dannie had returned happily to school that week; Shelly had an hour to steady herself before he came home. Sheina was shopping and Greg out in the fields. She savoured her new skill. What she had done once, she could do again. Even the physiotherapist would be astonished if she knew.

For the first time she let herself think ahead.

Jamie had become important to her, but she did not want him to know that. There was no way she was going to tie him to a woman who was crippled and would be a big responsibility. If she could walk, then everything would change. She intended to keep him at a distance until she was sure. She would walk. She could stand . . . she could feel some sensation in her legs. It was painful, but it was a sign of life.

For the first time since the accident she felt excitement and hope. Now, when she was alone in the house, with Sheina busy around the farm and Greg out with the sheep, she called Star to fetch her rope.

Progress was slow, but by the end of the month she could count to ten before her legs betrayed her. One morning Star moved backwards, still tugging, pulling Shelley forwards. She took one step. Movement was agonizing, bringing long-unused muscles back to life, screaming in protest, but she was determined. So was Star, who seemed to understand just how long each game should last.

It became a new hope to cherish. Star seemed to encourage her, so that each day there was a fractional improvement. The tiniest sign of a possible future. Nobody else was to know. This remained a secret. If she failed, no one would guess how she had struggled. They had expected nothing, and would not be disappointed. Only she would know that she had tried, and failed.

Failure was unthinkable.

Star was teaching her determination. She would succeed. And then . . .

Fifteen

Star never stopped learning, and often she seemed to think for herself.

'A miracle dog,' Jamie said, watching her one evening as she worked out how to extricate a pen he had hidden under a chair. After several attempts to get it, she lay on her side, reached out her paw and flipped it. It came out sideways. She picked it up to take to Shelley.

A moment later the pups, bored and in need of occupation, decided to take it from their mother. Before Star realized what had happened, Amber had it in her mouth. Hero tried to take it from her, causing his sister growl at him. Both quailed before their mother who turned on them, snarling, picked up the abandoned pen and took it, as she had intended, to Shelley. Hero and Amber went to their beds.

Neither would challenge Star again.

'She manages her pups much better than I manage mine,' Shelley said.

The pair, growing rapidly, had as much character as Star though all three were very different. Star had immense confidence, though she was still wary of unknown men, watching them from a distance, refusing to approach them.

Hero was an explorer, and also apt to pick up very unsuitable objects, unable to resist the drive born in him for retrieving game. Greg did not appreciate being brought chicks soaked in saliva, and neither did the chicks. Even though the hen flew at him, he often seemed to find a straggler.

It was some time before Greg realized the dog was bringing him tiny birds that were lost, and had not taken them from their mother. Within days Hero had a new job, and he and Greg searched the yard and the nearby fields, looking for strays. He was the dog that barked at intruders; Rab seemed to have abdicated. Meg dozed through her days.

Amber was the most affectionate, needing human contact, always leaning against a leg, looking up with soulful eyes pleading for petting. Hero liked a brisk pat, Amber a long cuddle. Mostly they were easy biddable little animals, full of fun, romping and playing in the yard.

They were also full of mischief. It was some time before they could be trusted on their own as Greg had to teach them not to chase the poultry. He managed to persuade them that hens and ducks were not fair game. The geese gave a far tougher lesson than their owner and soon convinced the pair that racing after them was going to end in a very unpleasant experience.

There were times when even Sheina vowed to find the pups a new home.

One morning Hero found Greg's new shoes and took them outside. He decided it would be interesting to put them in the duck pond. They were soaked and muddy and had teeth marks in them when Sheina found them. She was not enchanted. Nor was their owner.

Amber followed Sheina round all morning while she planted out the new tubs that they had bought to brighten up the approach to the farm shop. Unwisely, she left the pair outside. What could be put in could very easily be pulled out and some time later Shelley, wheeling herself outside, saw a scene of chaos. Every single plant had been uprooted and laid on the ground.

Training began to take effect as the months passed, but there were still days when both seemed possessed of a demon of naughtiness.

'Can't expect old heads on young shoulders,' Greg said one afternoon with a sigh after a long search for his screwdriver, which Hero had carried off when he laid it down. Shelley sent Star to find it, and she brought to him.

'I wish I'd thought to ask her before wasting all that time.'

'They're so different to the collies,' Sheina said. 'We forget what she can do.'

'Star seems to be teaching Dannie as well as Hero and Amber,' Shelley said one evening. She now sat with her parents after Dannie had gone to bed, instead of retreating to her own room. 'Have you noticed she always goes to him when he gets upset, and nudges him till he pets her? And forgets whatever it was that was bothering him.'

'The pups are good for him,' Greg said.

'They're all three good for all of us,' Shelley said, thinking of her well-kept secret. She could now walk three steps, using a stick in one hand and holding the tug in the other, Star pulling determinedly.

The farm shop was now fun, meeting new people, who forgot she was in a wheelchair. Everyone wanted to fuss Star.

'If only she could talk,' Jamie said one day. 'She'd have a tale to tell, I suspect.'

'She's got a tail to wag,' Dannie said, laughing.

Greg was sitting in his armchair with a couple of sandwiches on a plate on his knee. Hero, seizing an opportunity, grabbed one. Star's bark caused him to drop it.

She picked it up and brought it back to Greg, who tried not to laugh.

'Thank you, Star,' he said taking it from her, and winking at Dannie. 'Though somehow I don't really fancy it.'

He put it on the side of his plate.

'We'd better save it for the hens. I can't give it to Star and Hero most certainly isn't going to benefit from his theft.'

'Is there anything that dog can't do?' Jamie asked a few weeks later, after collecting Dannie from school. This had gradually become a habit; Jamie would pick the boy up on his rounds and drop him off; time for a chat and a slice of cake before returning to take surgery. Dannie always felt let down if Jamie had an emergency and couldn't bring him home after all.

'She can't talk, though she can certainly communicate. I sometimes think she'll be offering me sandwiches next,' Shelley said, laughing. 'Not sure I'd eat them, though, even though she is a very clean dog.'

It was almost September again. The holidays were busier than ever as Dannie's school friends were always wanting to see Star. Their parents, equally fascinated, came too, which meant many more customers for Sheina's cream teas.

Star had been with them for almost eighteen months when Jamie called in early one evening, complete with a large pizza, which turned their teatime into a party. His visits invariably began in chaos as Star and her pups now raced to him, and Dannie followed, eager to greet him. Meg was ageing fast and rarely did more than wag her tail and Rab preferred always to be with Greg.

Star lay at Shelley's feet, watching them eat the pizza. Dannie, on a stool beside his mother's chair, was slipping the dog tiny pieces of his own share, hoping nobody would notice. Greg and Sheina had finished work and were sharing the treat.

The phone rang and Star brought it across to Greg.

'Feed delivery tomorrow,' he said, as he rang off. Star took the phone from him and returned it to its stand.

'She really is clever,' Jamie said. 'I don't know if it's the way she was trained, or that she's a most exceptionally intelligent dog.'

'A combination of both, I'd imagine,' Greg said. He had been amazed over and over again by Star's skills. 'I'm not sure that her pups aren't brighter than she is. I spend so little time on them yet they pick everything up so fast.'

'I wish we know where she came from and had her pedigree,' Shelley said. 'Her pups could be trained too, and might be as good as she is. We could offer them to one of the societies that train dogs for the disabled.'

'You could breed again from her next year,' Jamie said. 'If we find the right dog we could produce some incredible pups. I doubt if the lack of her pedigree would matter if you trained them before selling them on.'

'Me train them?' Shelley stared at him, convinced he had lost his wits.

'Why not? You helped train your dad's sheepdogs. It's the same principle, whatever the dog does in the end. Hamish Grant won the local sheepdog trials three years ago, working his dog from a wheelchair.'

'Don't get carried away. The pedigree does matter,' Greg said. 'Suppose she carries an inherited fault, and we choose the wrong dog? There's always a chance of blindness or bad hips, or even epilepsy, coming from long ago and meeting in the pups. It can happen after so many generations. Look at the Brunts' red calf.'

'That was a panic,' Jamie said, laughing.

'Why?' Dannie asked.

His grandfather smiled at him. The boy had changed so much in the past few months. He was interested in everything about him and enjoyed sharing the chores when he was at home.

'The Brunts have Friesians, which are black and white,' Greg said. 'One day they woke up to find a cow had produced a red and white calf and thought that somebody else's bull must have got in. They'd used the same bull on all the cows, so that was worrying too. Perhaps he wasn't a pure bred animal. They looked up the history of the Friesians and discovered that when they first came here, some hundreds of years ago, they could be red and white or black and white. It had come from all those years back.'

Star was sitting beside him, looking into his face, as if she understood every word.

He laughed and patted her.

'It's a risk. I don't think it's an option. I wouldn't be happy.'

On the Saturday after Dannie's eighth birthday they had a party. He didn't want any of his school friends. He'd seen plenty of them during the holidays and now he saw them every day at school. He wanted Jamie and Angus and Jamie's mother and his own grandparents. David's parents were invited, but could not face the eleven-hour journey. They sent cards and a large cheque and a small bicycle.

Shelley made a cake, and iced it.

Star might be the cleverest dog in the world, but she still sat hopefully beside anyone who was cooking, or eating, hoping for crumbs to drop.

Dannie's presents were to be opened when the visitors came. His excitement spilled over. Jamie piled them in a corner. This was his show. His mother had never seen Star display her abilities. The dog sat, watching everyone in turn, aware that this was an unusual occasion.

Jamie led her to the pile of presents. He handed her the top one.

'Give it to Dannie.'

Star took it in her mouth and trotted across the room. She laid her offering on Dannie's knees.

'Wait,' Jamie said.

She sat, tongue hanging out, eyes alight with interest until the contents had been explored and Jamie said,

'Now another one. Fetch.'

This was a fascinating game. She soon realized she had to sit still until Dannie had opened his gift, and then, the minute he put the paper in the basket beside him and admired his new toy, she sped across the room to bring the next.

Some of the wrapping paper had fallen on the floor. Star picked it up and put it in the waste paper basket. She lay quietly while everyone ate.

'Impressed?' Jamie asked his mother, who had been watching the dog with some astonishment.

'She's magnificent,' she said. 'A real showstopper. Look at the gleam on that coat.'

'Can't show her without a pedigree,' Jamie said. 'It's a pity. Shelley could have a lot of fun.'

'In a wheelchair?' Shelley said. 'You must be joking. And how would I get there?'

'I've seen a wheelchair in the ring,' Angus said. 'You can drive. You can apply for a specially adapted car. You don't have to sit here and go nowhere unless someone can take you.'

Shelley sighed.

'No way. There's no point anyway as we don't know her background. We can't show her in Breed classes without a pedigree. It's a pity. I'm sure she'd do well.'

'You could train her for Obedience. You can even enter crossbreeds for that. All you do is put on the entrance form "parentage unknown". Dannie could handle her. Come to that, I could take him. I've always enjoyed shows.'

Dannie looked at his mother, excitement in his eyes.

'Can we go to shows? With Star?'

'Not with Star,' Greg said. 'Your mother needs her. But what about Amber? We can train Hero as well. You can start with little shows, and maybe later try some of the big ones. There aren't many round here, but there are a few.'

Shelley did not want to go with them. There was always

the problem of inadequate wheelchair access, especially for toilets. Those at show venues were often makeshift, just a tent or a caravan. Jamie promised to make notes so that if it was possible she could come too. He and Dannie went off by themselves. Dannie found these excursions exciting and was enchanted when he was chosen as Best Junior Handler at four little shows.

His red rosettes had pride of place on the kitchen wall.

'I want as many as you, Grandad,' he said one morning, looking at the big kitchen dresser in the farmhouse which was almost hidden under Greg's trophies.

Sheina was endlessly busy. Farm holidays were popular and she was full up to the end of October. Shelley did not need her so much, as Star had come into her own: she was extra hands and extra eyes and extra ears. Jamie and Greg both took turns at training the pups to follow her. Both might one day be sold, though Greg doubted if that were possible. They could not bear to part with them. The little family had stolen their own way into the household.

'Do you think . . .?' Sheina said one day, looking out of the window. Jamie was playing ball with Star, who adored fetching it. Shelley laughed when one of his throws sent the ball into a tree. Star stood on her hind legs. She couldn't reach it. She jumped and shook the branch where it was wedged.

It fell to the ground and she picked it up, running happily to Jamie. He threw it again and then went to talk to Shelley. The two heads were close together. 'Shelley's so much more relaxed. She enjoys their picnics and Dannie's fishing expeditions.'

'Up to them,' Greg said, knowing her hopes. It was close to three years since David had died. He could wish, but he would never interfere. Life had improved so much since he found Star and her pups. If only it would continue.

Sixteen

Dannie had given his mother a diary the previous Christmas. At first it remained unused, but as the tugging sessions progressed, Shelley began to write in it. Brief notes, but they told her all she needed and when she felt depressed at her slow progress, she could look back and see for herself that she was making headway.

That first day she had written, 'Star tugged me to my feet! I stood and counted three.'

Then, a month later, 'I stood and counted a hundred.'

And then in huge capitals: 'I WALKED TWO STEPS.'

The days suddenly had point to them. There was so much more she could do with Star at her side. The dog seemed to consider herself her guardian.

Shelley had a special bath with a hoist to help her in, and Star hated bath time. Sheina timed it meticulously. Shelley had half an hour. It worried Star to see Shelley lying there, and to be unable to reach her. She sat, as if on duty, watching every movement. Hopefully, she brought the towels and dropped them at the bath side when Shelley refused to take them, wanting to lie still longer and revel in the bliss of hot water. The dog was obviously relieved when at last Shelley was dry and dressed and back in her wheelchair.

Meg now slept away her days, waking briefly to feed, to greet those she loved, and to take brief sorties outside. She no longer had the energy to help Sheina herd the chickens safely into their roosting boxes at night.

Star not only took over but seemed to know the time, nudging Sheina if she were not ready, and then rounding up the chickens and herding them across the yard, never missing one.

She was a vocal dog, who made Dannie laugh when she

began her small grunts. These were soft chatty sounds, but if no one noticed her they escalated, ending finally in a frustrated bark, as if she were saying, 'Look. I'm here. Give me something to do.'

She helped Dannie get ready for school, bringing him his school bag. When it was heavy she dragged it across the floor. She brought his trainers, and found his gym shoes and kit.

Shelley was never up at this time. At first Dannie did not realize that this had become a daily occurrence, and when he did, he couldn't wait to tell his mother.

'She even knows when it's Saturday and Sunday,' he said. 'She never brings me my school things then.'

That explained a minor mystery. Shelley often wondered why Star stayed beside her every weekend, but left her early on weekdays, to return only after Dannie had left for school.

There was more work to do during the holiday season, and their bed and breakfast rooms were fully booked. Star always warned them of newcomers in the yard, and ran out to greet the visitors. Rab was usually out with Greg, and the pups now had a pen in the yard as they were apt to get into trouble. Hero in particular had an exploring streak in him and would, if not watched, take off down the lane. If Star were there she brought him back, snapping at his heels. But after it had happened twice, Greg built an enclosure. There was too much risk of the dog being run over, and in any case a wandering dog was not a good idea. Especially in sheep country.

Greg had made a notice that read, 'If no one answers the doorbell please call in the farm shop.'

Most of the produce in the greenhouse attached to the shop was watered mechanically, but there were a few ornamental plants which Shelley tended, using a small watering can that was not too heavy when filled.

Star took the empty can to the tap for her. It was another shared chore, made infinitely less dreary by the dog's assistance. She could also hold the trug while Shelley picked the produce. Visitors to the shop were always fascinated.

Although Sheina made sure there was plenty to sell, they often ran out towards closing time, and then Star came into her own, always eager to play her part, always certain this was just another exciting game.

One day an elderly visitor dropped her purse. Star picked it up, and offered it to its owner.

'You'll be teaching her to count the change,' the visitor said, laughing, 'Aren't you lucky to have her?'

You don't know how lucky, Shelley thought. The tug game was progressing, and the effort was bringing back disused muscles that still protested violently when she took a step, but that was a sign of improvement. She learned that she must be careful not to overdo any session, as that meant she was unable to move for several days afterwards.

She could now take her weight on her arms and lower herself gently into the chair instead of falling painfully down with a bump that jarred her.

One morning Star was unusually persistent, barking constantly, trying to attract attention from either Sheina or Greg. Mystified, they checked the yard, and even went round to the front door of the farmhouse, which nobody ever used.

She kept running towards the big five-barred gate, turning her head, as if inviting them to follow. There was no sign of any car in the lane. She did not usually pester them in this way. She had a well worked out routine that everyone knew, but today was definitely different. Something was bothering her.

Greg went to the gate, which led out into a narrow lane, bordered by wide grass verges. He was always meaning to cut them but there was never enough time. He heard a faint noise, and opened the gate and walked out. There was a large cardboard box in the long grass.

Inside were four black kittens, not more than three weeks old. They looked up at him out of terrified baby blue eyes. Somewhere a mother cat was grieving. Somewhere were people who had dumped their responsibility. Anger flared as he lifted the box, walked inside, and closed the gate.

'Another job for you and Shelley,' Greg said, as Star followed him across the yard into the kitchen, where Sheina was making coffee. He put the box on the floor and opened it. Star thrust her nose in and was met by four small mouths that hissed and spat.

'What was bothering Star?' Shelley asked, wheeling herself in for her coffee break, as there were no customers.

Greg pointed to the box.

'Someone left us a present. Star must have heard them crying. Good job she did. They look pretty feeble. I wonder how long they were out there?'

'They left them during the night. Star wouldn't settle. She kept roaming the room and going to the window, and making her funny little grunts. I was so tired I got cross with her. They don't look very healthy. Will they survive? How old are they? People . . . I hate them sometimes,' Shelley said.

Sheina was busy diluting evaporated milk, looking for medicine droppers, and finding Rescue Remedy. Star lay by the box as if on guard, ensuring nobody harmed the newcomers. An hour later the kittens were fed. Star licked each one, cleaning it as if it were a puppy. Then she picked each kit up, carried it to the rug and lay down beside them cuddling them up against her. They were as yet too young to know real fear, and her warm body comforted them. They burrowed into her fur.

Sheina rang Jamie, asking him to bring kitten milk when he brought Dannie home. Shelley had a new responsibility. The kittens needed feeding every three hours. They would need night time feeds for a week, Jamie said, when he saw them.

He brought a small cage, so that Shelley could keep them beside her in the farm shop. The feeds were adjusted. Greg fed them at midnight, and then Sheina set her alarm clock for four a.m. which meant Shelley could sleep through the night and take over at eight.

Star added the kittens to her charges. She knew when it was feed time and as they began to run around she watched over them as devotedly as any mother cat.

Hero and Amber both knew that kittens were not for chasing, though the kittens, as they grew and began to have freedom, teased the dogs, enticing them to run.

The barn cats accepted them but ignored them.

The visitors loved them, and once they were old enough, homes were easily found. Star haunted the gate for a time, as if hoping for more refugees.

139

Then, to everyone's amusement, one of the barn cats had kittens and Star became a proxy mother, again quite happy to take over babysitting duties.

'She needs another litter,' Jamie said, watching her cuddle up to four tiny mites who seemed to think she was a trampoline. 'A litter she can rear with our help, and that will satisfy that maternal instinct.'

It seemed as if pups would be a good idea.

'Maybe we could mate her to a Labrador and then we wouldn't run the risk of inherited faults,' Greg said.

'It's an idea,' Jamie said. 'The Guide Dog people do it all the time. It's a very good cross. Sound, intelligent, and mostly carries the best qualities of both breeds.'

'Maybe next year,' Greg said. 'Shelley needs her and if she's busy with pups she'll be distracted.'

Every day now, Shelley insisted on an hour to herself. To read and think, she said, and gather strength for the day.

In fact she needed the time for the tugging game, which now took longer, and was beginning to show such good results that excitement built in her. She couldn't wait for morning, for Star to dance across the room, her rope in her mouth and then the insistent pull, punctuated by small grunts.

Stand and count. Get her breath. Listen to Star who she felt was saying, 'Come on. You can do it. Come on.'

Then Star began to back away, across the room. Every day, just one step more, almost as if the dog had been programmed. Each day she progressed just one step and stood for longer, though as yet she could not yet stand without holding on to a support.

Life settled into a good routine. Nobody could imagine being without Star and Hero and Amber, both now steadying into sensible dogs. Dannie spent much of his time teaching them.

'He loves it,' Greg said one afternoon, watching Dannie walk Hero through his paces. 'It's a great hobby. I've promised to teach him to work Rab. He's growing into a great little helper, our Dannie.'

The farm was prospering, the farm shop making record sales as holidaymakers flocked into the area. The bed and breakfast rooms were always full, and everyone enjoyed the visitors. Dannie loved talking to them, especially any who came from overseas. One day he was going to backpack round the world.

Life had become exciting, with the shows to look forward to – just once a month as Jamie was busy, and was always needed on hand to back Dannie up.

Hero was not yet doing well at any but the tiny shows. Winning Junior Handler was easy, but to work the dog in the obedience routines was much more difficult. Dannie wanted what he called real red rosettes, not just those from shows where there was very little competition.

His confidence was growing with every new success, however small, and Jamie encouraged him. So did Greg, who found that the child loved helping on the farm and was becoming a big asset, able to take over small tasks, like egg collecting, with Star's help. Sheina was able to find time for some of the harder tasks, and this in turn freed Greg.

Dannie's first win of any significance came, unexpectedly, not at a dog show but at the big Agricultural show. Greg had no time to show any of his animals, but Jamie drove Dannie, having helped him prepare his one ram lamb, which took first prize.

Dannie exploded when he came home, dancing round the room, holding up the red rosette. Star barked at him, as if telling him to quell his excitement.

'Next time it'll be Hero,' he said. 'He's getting on a treat, isn't he, Grandad?'

There was a big show about forty miles away at the end of October and Jamie had promised to get the day off and take Dannie and his dog. There was time for practice, for Jamie to come over and watch Dannie and correct his mistakes. Hero was developing a desire to work, and never took his eyes off his small handler.

Dannie practised in the yard, intriguing the visitors.

Shelley often sat with Star, watching. Maybe one day she would be able to walk and could work Star and go with Dannie to some of the nearer shows.

'You'll be at Crufts yet,' one of the visitors said, only half teasing.

Dannie looked up at him.

'I know,' he said, quite sure that he and Hero were going to shine together and there would be many more red rosettes to vie with his grandad's on the kitchen wall. He wanted to train Amber too, but Jamie pointed out that it was better to concentrate on her brother, as his attention would otherwise be divided.

Amber, meanwhile, was watching her mother, and had begun also to pick things up and bring them to whoever owned them.

The day the ram won his prize was also a red letter day for Shelley too. She stood for the first time without holding on to the back of the chair for support, or using Star to tug her up.

The October show was only three weeks away and summer was turning into autumn, which painted the leaves with spectacular colour, when the last of the year's visitors came to stay.

Paul and Della Manville bred Golden Retrievers. They arrived late in the evening and did not meet Star or her pups. Next morning, Shelley took the three into the yard and they began to play just as the Manvilles finished breakfast. They came out to watch, intrigued to find so many Goldens.

'Did you breed them?' Della asked, and then stared.

Star was carrying the phone to Shelley, who was sitting in her wheelchair in the kitchen doorway.

'We found—' Greg began, but was interrupted as Della said,

'Paul. Look!'

Star offered the phone to Shelley, who took it from her and began to talk to the caller. At the sound of new voices the dog turned towards the visitors with a faint air of puzzlement, her tail weaving slowly.

'I'd swear . . .'

Della was sure.

'Star,' she called. 'Here, Star girl. Let's look at you.'

It was a familiar voice. Star ran across to the newcomers, her tail frantic. She greeted them with joy.

Greg, walking across the farmyard, stood quite still, hoping his worst fear had not been realized.

'I'm sure it's Star,' Paul said. 'Her owner brought her over

142

from Anglesey to mate with our champion, Siegfried. They spent a week with us. She was stolen, just before the pups were due, by thugs who wrecked the house. That was, when? Two years ago next February. We all thought she was dead.'

'I found her with her pups on the hills,' Greg said. 'She must have escaped.'

The timing was right. The Manvilles had no doubts.

'We must phone Matt and Liz. They'll be overjoyed to know she's safe,' Paul said.

'Anglesey is a very long way away,' Greg said, afraid his dismay would show in his face. 'How in the world would she have got here? Are you sure it is the dog you knew?'

'With a name like Star? And she definitely remembers us.'

There was no doubt about that.

Greg looked across the yard at Shelley who was staring at him, utter misery in her face. They would take Star and her pups away, to return them to their rightful owners, and she would be bereft. She could not bear the thought.

What about Hero and Amber?

How would she tell Dannie?

It was the end of all their hopes.

Seventeen

Far away in Anglesey Matt Grey was about to switch on the television for the evening news and weather report when the phone rang.

'Della Manville!' he said in surprise as the caller identified herself. 'I didn't expect to hear from you.'

He had told the Manvilles about Star's disappearance and they had been almost as upset as her owners. Like them, they expected so much of her pups. One little bitch from her litter had been booked instead of a stud fee.

'We're in Scotland,' Della said. 'Right up in the Highlands. On holiday. You'll never guess, Matt. The people here have Star. They found her and two pups on the hills in the snow and gave her a home. It's a very good home. She's in wonderful condition. And she recognized us.'

Star. He couldn't believe it. She was well. He could see her again. He could bring her back where she belonged. Have another litter from her next year. He wondered if she had forgotten all he taught her. Did her new owners realize how exceptional she was?

'I can't wait to see. Do you think she'll remember her old name? What have they called her?'

'That's quite extraordinary. They've called her Star.'

How did they know her name? Immediate suspicion crossed his mind. The rest of the conversation passed in a blur. He took the address of the farm and the phone number and went to find Liz.

'Scotland?' Liz stared at him. 'How in the world did she get there? She *must* have been stolen, but how did she get away?'

Matt couldn't wait to see Star. He rang back that evening and identified himself to Sheina. He arranged for them to

144

come the following weekend and stay for at least couple of days. They would take Star and her pups home with them. Matt and Liz were retired, so there were no commitments to prevent them travelling when they chose.

They had no doubts whatever that her new owners would surrender stolen property.

Sheina listened to Matt's excited voice. It was unbearable. She did not tell Greg of the booking until Shelley had gone to bed. She had hoped that Star's previous owners would have given up and not want her back. She knew it was a faint hope, and most unlikely. The Greys obviously wanted her back. The certainty of their own loss plunged her into despair. It would devastate Dannie and Shelley.

'How do we tell them?' she asked.

'There's no easy way. They'll both be distraught. They adore the dogs . . . as we do.'

Neither of them slept much that night.

Next day was Saturday. No school. Greg did not know if that made the news easier to give or worse. He told his daughter and grandson, before they left the breakfast table, that Star's real owners would be coming to collect her and the pups.

Though they were no longer pups, the name stuck. Both had matured into handsome animals, with all their mother's charisma.

'No. No. No. No.' Dannie kicked his feet against the table leg. 'They can't have her. They can't.'

Della and Paul Manville, about to come into the room for their breakfast, having planned to leave early, overheard the yells. They looked at one another in dismay and decided to wait. Instead, they went outside into the yard. Toffee came to greet them, hoping for a crust of bread. Disappointed, she wandered off, one of the barn kittens following her.

'There's going to be heartache,' Della said. 'I didn't think . . . I wish we hadn't told them. Matt does have Lisa now, and he must have almost forgotten Star.' Lisa was Star's half sister, born a year later, given by her breeder to Matt and Liz to make up for their loss. But although Matt had spent a great deal of time training the pup, she lacked Star's qualities.

145

'I doubt it,' her husband said. 'She's a one-in-a-million dog. And when you've had one like that nothing else ever quite comes up to it. There's always a lurking core of disappointment, of feeling cheated because no other dog is as good. I've never had another dog like Miracle.'

He sighed. Miracle was long ago, a champion who had once worked in Obedience at Crufts. He had come second. The dog of a lifetime.

The conversation in the kitchen was not going well.

Dannie was reduced from temper to tears. Shelley stared at Greg. Life couldn't do that to her. She couldn't lose Star. Not now. Star was her lifeline, her passport to the future. Star gave her both support and confidence.

Star was her companion, keeping away the loneliness that had engulfed her since David died. Star was her reassurance in the long sleepless nights, coming the instant Shelley called, always there for her, her warm body curled in the armchair beside the bed, her head on Shelley's shoulder, her soft tongue licking away tears.

Without Star she would never be able to walk again. Life would become far more difficult, having to do everything without help. Losing Star would affect all of them. Shelley would be dependent again on her mother, who would have less time to help on the farm. No other dog would understand what was wanted. They had added so much to Star's repertoire. No other dog could ever replace her.

Dannie was doing so well with Hero. That was another dream blighted.

Shelley sat silent, her face white, unable to believe in such bad luck. My fault, she thought. If I hadn't been so ambitious and made Mum and Dad start the bed and breakfast, the Manvilles would never have come.

Sheina was just as upset. She had no comfort to give. They would lose a way of life if they lost Star, and she did not see how they could refuse to give her back. She was, after all, stolen property. She thought, idiotically, of a rhyme that she had made up when their favourite sheepdog died. Shelley was a little older than Dannie then, but had grieved for weeks. Death was too frequent a part of farm life, but even so, there was always the emptiness and the dreadful ache when one of their treasured animals died. One of the worst of all had been the loss of Greg's hoped-for champion, far too young. The collie had won several sheepdog trials and Greg hoped for great things.

Maxie died at five of a heart attack. Nobody had known he had been born with a heart defect. He had meant more to them than any of their other dogs. And now they were going to suffer the same way with Star.

Sheina had written in her diary then. She remembered the words too well.

> There are many sorts of hell as most of us know full well.
> But the worst of them all for me is the time there has to
> be
> When you are forced to part with the dog that owns half
> your heart.

She suddenly realized there was something worse. They were going to lose a lifeline, but not to death. This would be harder to accept. Also all three dogs would go. She had to watch Shelley and Dannie suffer and know nothing she could do or say would help. She wished that Greg had not found Star and her pups. She would rather they were dead.

'They can't have her,' Dannie said through his tears. 'They can't.'

'We can't stop them,' Greg said. 'She's legally theirs. I'll try and buy her from them, but . . .'

He shrugged. Of all the bad luck. Why did the Manvilles have to pick their farm for their holiday? Hadn't Fate done enough to blight their lives? A memory of last week's sermon came to him, the minister, a man of fire, declaiming loudly from the pulpit. 'Man is born to trouble as the sparks fly upwards.'

'They didn't look after her,' Dannie insisted. 'They don't deserve her.'

'Dannie, she was stolen. They loved her as much as we do. They must have been so unhappy when they found her gone. They were looking forward to her puppies. They had no idea what had happened to her, whether she was dead, or with people who were mistreating her. At least we'll know she's back with people who love her and is in a very good home.'

He knew his attempt at being reasonable was not going to help Dannie, who stormed out of the room, slamming the door behind him, sure that nobody else really cared. He called Hero and went out into the yard. There was a tiny corner behind the barn, a secret den, that only he and the dog knew. He curled up, soaking the dog with his tears. He couldn't live without his dogs.

The Manvilles watched in dismay, and went indoors, unable to voice their unhappiness. They had been so delighted to find Star alive and well. Now they wished they had never found her.

'I think we'll skip breakfast and get it on the way,' Paul said. 'We can go out the front way. I'll leave the money on the dressing table. They won't want to face us. We've tossed a grenade into their lives.'

Nobody heard them leave, feeling almost criminal.

Sheina had forgotten the visitors. She looked at the slammed door, and stood up to follow her grandson.

'Leave him,' Greg said. 'Nothing we can do will help.'

He wanted to hug Dannie. He wanted time to roll backwards, so that the Manvilles had never come. No use agonizing. It wasn't going to help. They'd get over it in time. Meanwhile it was painful to see the dogs running around, unaware that everything in their lives had changed.

Jamie, arriving late, took Dannie out for a walk. He did not want to go. He couldn't face the day, knowing that Star and her pups would soon be gone.

Everyone kept busy. That way, there was no time to brood. Shelley shut her door. She couldn't bear to look at Star or have her near. She tried to sew, but pricked her finger.

Sheina forgot to collect the eggs until Star reminded her. The dog was baffled by the odd behaviour of all the humans. Greg took Rab and checked the sheep for foot rot, but his thoughts kept drifting away from his task.

It was worse when Dannie came home. He was edgy and angry and reluctant to do anything he was told. Sheina kept him busy until their evening meal. Nobody felt hungry.

Next day was even worse. Dannie refused to eat. He refused

to help. He yelled at his mother when she asked him to shut the door, which he had left open, as there was a gale blowing through from a rising wind that made the dogs edgy.

He stamped off to bed still shouting.

'I hate you all. You won't do anything. You'll just let them come and take them all away. You don't care. I'll never get to Crufts now. Hero's mine. They can't have him.'

The week following was quiet. They might have casual callers who had not booked, but at the moment they were free. Sheina had had no heart to tidy up after the Manvilles left but now she had to make the effort. They had not said goodbye. There was a note under the envelope containing their money.

'We're so sorry. But we had to tell them she's safe and well. They have been so unhappy, not knowing where she was or what had happened to her or if she'd been killed that night.'

She sighed as she looked out of the window. Star was sitting in the yard, forlorn. Nobody was taking any notice of her. Sheina had the beds to change, the linen and towels to wash, the rooms to clean. Dannie fetched and carried, protesting all the time, the aura of his presence revealing a seething storm that he could barely contain.

He had no intention of giving up. The argument resumed as soon as the dishes were cleared that evening. He had promised Jamie he wouldn't lose his temper and make matters worse, but his feelings mastered him. Greg wondered why it was that Jamie and Angus had so much more influence over his grandson than they did.

'They're all as upset as you are, Dannie,' Jamie said before he went back to take evening surgery. 'Don't make it worse for your Mum. She minds as much as you do.'

And she'll suffer much more, he thought. Star did so much for her. Without her, Shelley would find life difficult again.

Jamie left. Dannie felt betrayed and heartbroken. Star and Hero and Amber were to leave them for ever. Nobody understood how he felt. If his mother cared she'd help him find a way to keep the dogs. So she didn't care. All she said was that Star wasn't theirs. Nor were her pups. Of course they was theirs.

He didn't see his mother's tears, or understand that Shelley felt as if her world had ended all over again.

As far as Dannie was concerned, grownups were there to put things right, not to let wrong things happen. They'd sorted out Paul, once he'd told them. Grandad could buy Star. Or hide her, or pretend he'd sold her. They didn't have to let her go. They just weren't listening, weren't thinking.

He wanted to scream at them, to kick them, to pummel his mother out of her apathy, make her respond to him, make her want to do things again, make her try to walk. She could, some part of him had never stopped believing, if she tried. Her legs were still there.

There was no way he could stay silent.

It became a litany that he repeated over and over as if hoping his words might change everything. It added to the misery that everyone else felt. Shelley thought that if he said it again she would scream.

'You don't care. None of you. If you did you'd do something to stop them. They can't take her. I won't let them,' he shouted. 'They'll want Amber and Hero too. I hope they never get here. I hope they crash. Not a bad one, but one that stops them coming. Ever.'

'Dannie . . .' Greg was at a loss for words.

'It's not fair. They didn't want her. They didn't look after her. They didn't find her when she got lost. They didn't bother. I won't let them take her.'

It was impossible to reason with him. Dannie was determined not to listen.

Nobody could pacify him. He cried so much that at last he was exhausted. Greg went in to say goodnight. The stormy tears were reduced to occasional sobs but Dannie didn't answer his grandfather. He pulled the covers over his head.

'I see breakers ahead,' Greg said the next evening to Sheina. Matt and Liz were due next day.

'Not breakers. Coral reefs. This is going to set us back years. Dannie's still so vulnerable. Shelley was beginning to be more like her old self. I don't know what this will do to her. I wish . . .'

Shelley didn't want to talk to anyone. If she did she would

break down into tears. She stayed in her room and refused to play the tugging game There was no point.

Star, bewildered, was subdued, and restless, looking anxiously from one face to the other as if afraid she had transgressed and was the cause of this strange atmosphere.

Shelley ate because her mother sat with her and nagged her until she managed at least a portion of what was on her plate.

'I could get over her dying,' she said next evening when Jamie brought a rebellious Dannie home. Picking him up from school and understanding everyone was exhausted by his tantrums, Jamie had taken him out for a long drive, hoping that viewing the rugged scenery would distract him. When they came back the boy rushed in from the yard, into his own room, taking Hero with him and shutting the door firmly behind him.

'This . . . it's so cruel. They've been ours for over two years.'

Shelley knew she was being unreasonable but that made no difference.

Jamie had nothing to say that would help. He would try and get another dog for her from one of the societies, but it wouldn't be the same. He wanted to stay and comfort her. He wanted to hold her and stroke her hair. He wanted to be with her, but she persisted in keeping him at a distance, uneasy in his presence.

He had thought, there on the river bank, that he had made progress and she had lowered her defences, but they were back again. If only he had more time, but the job got in the way.

'It's good in a way to find out where she came from,' Greg said to Jamie as he was going out of the door into the yard. 'But I wish we hadn't.'

The vet had another thought.

'You found her on the hill. She can't have gone far from wherever the thieves brought her. She must have escaped from them. She could never have wandered from Anglesey to here. It's an eleven-hour drive. If she was lost she'd make for her own home. Have you considered there might be a puppy farm somewhere near?'

Greg looked at him, startled. He thought he knew the area well.

'Some of those abandoned farms . . . there are several well hidden in the hills. The police may be able to find it and stop them. If it's the people who took her they may have a cache of stolen property there too.'

He frowned, working out his line of thought.

'Of course they might just buy the bitches from the thieves. We have regular notices about stolen in-whelp bitches. They're going for gundogs and guard dogs and lurchers and greyhounds. Also the bull breeds. There are fighting rings involved as well. Dad's put up a notice in the surgery to warn people.'

'Might be an idea to have a chat with our local police,' Greg said. 'A bitch from Anglesey certainly didn't get here under her own steam.'

Sheina, putting fresh soap in the guest bathroom, stood in the doorway to check and make sure there was nothing else she had forgotten.

It was going to get worse. When Star met her first owners . . . There was no way any of them could disguise that losing the dog would be a terrible wrench. It would not be an easy few days. It was too long a journey to expect them to leave at once.

Star could not understand why her mistress was so unhappy, and pushed against her, looking up with worried eyes.

'You're so lucky,' Shelley told the dog. 'You never know the future. If only . . .'

But there was no way she could forget what the future held in store.

Eighteen

Matt and Liz had arrangements to make before they could come to Scotland. The journey would take around eleven hours, according to Della. They did not want to return next day. That would entail far too much driving.

'Shall we take Lisa?' Liz asked.

'Ruth'll look after her,' he said, referring to the breeder from whom they had bought Star, and who had given them Lisa to comfort them after Star's kidnapping. 'It's a long journey and it might not be easy to travel the two dogs together when they've only just met. Star may take time to re-settle. She's been away so long.'

He was unusually silent on the journey. They stopped at the motorway services near Preston for a quick snack.

Liz knew her husband well.

'What's bothering you?' she asked.

'How did Star get to Scotland? Do you really believe she could have lived free with pups to care for? And that there were only two pups? And how did they know her name was Star? It's not a usual name for a dog.'

'So what are you thinking?'

'The local paper had that article on Star, after we took her to the school and showed the children how clever she was. The couple have a disabled daughter. I think he stole the dog, and the burglary was a cover-up. Or he paid someone to steal her.'

'The police said other bitches had been taken. How would anyone in Scotland read a local Anglesey paper?'

'Some visitor could have brought it. There's something very fishy here. I'd believe in them choosing the same name if it had been something simple, like Jess or Bess, or Goldie. But Star? I think they took her and whelped her and sold the other pups. Most Goldens have between nine and eleven in a litter and Ruth's stock is prolific. Nine pups at five hundred pounds a time is a boost to any farm income.'

'Matt . . . Della says they're good people. Don't jump in with all guns blazing when we arrive. Please.'

'I never do. But if there are grounds I'll prosecute them for theft.'

'Why would they steal our property as well? The police said there had been other burglaries like ours.'

'They're hardly likely to find anyone honest to steal a dog. I doubt if they did it themselves. It would be theft to order. The thieves cashed in on the opportunity.'

Liz sighed. Once Matt got an idea in his head . . . they had lost good friends before now because of his genius for misunderstanding.

She had looked forward to seeing Star again, but now she almost dreaded it. She was afraid Matt would make a scene. How on earth could a man who was so patient with dogs be so stupid with people?

Meanwhile everyone at the farm was trying to cope with Dannie. Greg was increasingly worried. His grandson was determined, stubborn and unpredictable. He called the three dogs to him constantly, needing to touch them, hold them, derive comfort from their presence. He was irritable and did not sleep well.

He behaved once more as if he hated his mother. She was too distressed herself to cope with him. She couldn't manage without Star. A bleak future stretched ahead. She wished her father had never found the little family.

'Can't we tell them her name's something else and this isn't the dog we found? And they're not her pups.' Dannie asked. 'Or perhaps Jamie could take them till they've gone and we can say they ran away.'

Sheina tried to be reasonable, though it was hard.

'Darling, Star's their dog. They've been worrying about her all this time, thinking she was dead or maybe with someone cruel. We can't do that.'

Next morning when Shelley woke, Star was not there. It was seven thirty. She had overslept. They had evolved an unvarying routine which made life easier for everyone.

154

Dannie always came in at seven with his mother's early morning cup of tea, but there was no sign of him this day. It was a firm routine. As soon as Shelley was settled he took Star out. Sheina came at half past eight to give Shelley her breakfast in bed and then returned later to help her daughter dress. Nothing seemed to go right. She had slept badly, too miserable to rest.

Sheina had come in before Shelley went to sleep to tell her there had been a phone call the night before from Star's owners. Liz had developed a migraine and they had decided to break their journey. They would not now arrive until Thursday evening. That was still too soon.

Shelley lay waiting, her temper rising slowly, as she waited for someone to come. Seven thirty came with no sign of anyone. She then lay worrying about Dannie. Star was not on her rug. Shelley whistled, but no dog came. Maybe he had done as he threatened and run away with her. She needed to get into her wheelchair but as yet that was something she had not managed alone.

She did not want to ring for her mother. Sheina had too much to do. She wished that Star's owners had already come and they could get the parting over. Without Star, her attempts at standing would cease. She needed the dog both to help her and to motivate her. She had to try.

She could not yet stand unless Star tugged her out of her chair. But Star would soon be gone. She must make the effort. Worry about Dannie flared into near panic.

She had never tried to get from bed to chair without help from her mother or father. I can do it, she said, over and over, but was unable to still the niggling feeling that she was wrong. She would end in an ignominious heap on the floor.

Maybe she could stand, if she held to the bedhead. The chair was within reach and she pulled it closer to her with her pick-up stick. If she fell perhaps Dannie would hear her. If he was there. He was usually up and dressed by now. Nearly eight o'clock. Sheina would not come for another half hour.

She managed to pull herself up and out of the bed, and stood, holding tight to the bedhead, for a minute or so. It seemed a very big step from the bed to the wheelchair but she managed it, falling on to the seat. It took her a few minutes to regain her breath and stop shaking.

In spite of that she had a feeling of achievement. Her stupid legs. Why couldn't they obey her brain? But she could stand without Star's aid, so maybe she would walk in time . . . maybe . . .

She guided the chair into Dannie's room. The bed was empty, though the covers showed that he had slept there. Where had he gone? If only her mother or father would come. But both were outside tending to the animals. Then she heard a sound. She wheeled round to the other side of the room, and looked down. Dannie was lying on the bedside rug, his arms wrapped tightly round Star, imprisoning her, his duvet over both of them.

He was sobbing into the golden fur.

'Dannie!'

She needed to hug him, to get down beside him, to soothe away the tears. She choked back the anger she felt at her helplessness. Anger directed at herself and at David and that stupid decision that had changed their lives for ever. If only she could forget. It was going to be harder than ever now.

Dannie was dressed. He sat up. He was holding Star so tightly that he hurt her. The more she struggled to free herself, the tighter his grip. She licked away his tears, which produced a further flood.

The atmosphere bothered her. Her tail drooped, wagging slightly but without enthusiasm and she looked up at Shelley as if asking her what was wrong. Dannie released his grip. Star came across to Shelley as if apologizing for her absence moments before. She came hesitantly. Nothing felt normal now. Shelley didn't want to play with her. Dannie wasn't teaching Hero, or running out to romp with the dogs.

Dannie rubbed his hand across his eyes and shouted at his mother.

'I'll run away with Star and the pups and hide. When they can't find them they'll go away again and we can come back. I need only go into the attic. They won't go up there. Gran can feed us. She doesn't want them to go either.'

Shelley sighed.

There was a lump in her throat and tears threatened. If

only he would come to her, but he was behaving as he had when she first came home. Dannie glared at her, refusing to go near her. She was an enemy, thwarting him. Star, puzzled, looked from one to the other, as if wondering what was wrong.

'Why can't you see you need Star. She's your legs. She can get things you can't. I need Hero. There's the big show coming up, my first ever big show. Hero ought to win. We've worked so hard. Now we can't go and it's all wasted. Next week there won't be any Star. Or Amber, or Hero. Those horrible people will have taken them away. I hate them. It isn't fair. She's ours.'

Star looked up at Shelley, torn between the need to help and the awareness that Dannie also needed her. His face was dirty where he had rubbed the tears away. His mother ached for him.

She wanted, desperately, to get out of the chair and kneel beside him and hug him tightly. She wanted to assure him that Star and the pups would stay with them, but that was as impossible as their Jersey cow Toffee giving birth to a litter of piglets.

Jamie had invented a new game, with Toffee as mother of all kinds of peculiar creatures. He and Dannie vied to produce the silliest. The last time they had played it Jamie had reduced everyone to laughter by saying he was as likely to win the lottery as Toffee was to give birth to a butterfly.

Shelley stared out of the window. Not even the hills could comfort her. Their future had been wrecked. Dannie had improved so much in the past months. Now he was behaving appallingly, making sure everyone suffered with him.

She remembered her own childhood and wished she hadn't. It had taken her months to get over the death of her favourite pony. She had blamed everyone. Her father for not looking after her properly; Angus for not saving her life. It was years before she understood that Bracken had cancer, was very ill indeed and in pain and they had acted for the best.

But Star wasn't dying. She was being taken from them. Her owners would benefit from all the new skills she had learned. Shelley wondered if Liz too was disabled.

They couldn't change anything. Shelley had to learn to

survive all over again. She had cherished the hope that she would walk within the year, and then maybe she and Jamie . . .

She pushed the thought away. She was condemned to loneliness. It was impossible to argue with Dannie. She couldn't cope with him. She wheeled herself into the kitchen and made coffee and toasted a slice of bread, although she didn't feel like eating.

Sheina would help her dress later. She felt as if the dogs had suddenly been given just two days to live. For some reason this morning it felt worse than before. Parting was going to be horrendous for all of them. The Greys were due around seven the next evening. Then, next week, there would only be the two collies, and the most tremendous gap in their lives.

The pups would have to get used to a completely new routine, and were being taken to a completely new environment. She thought it likely the Greys would sell them. Perhaps she could buy them. The thought brought a crumb of comfort. She could salvage Dannie's show, even if she herself was going to feel as if a limb had been amputated. Amber was beginning to bring things when asked, but there was a long way to go before she would even begin to approach Star's usefulness.

Sheina came into the kitchen, startled to find Shelley out of bed.

'Did Dannie help you?' she asked.

'He'd taken Star into his room and shut the door. I thought he'd run away. I managed by myself.'

'That's great,' Sheina said.

She made herself toast and poured out a mug of coffee. She wished she had told the Greys that they were booked up, but had not thought of it in time. The dogs would be there for a couple more nights but Star might desert them completely once she was reunited with her real owners. The pups would not know them.

The weekend had been terrible. The next two days were worse, the time dragging. The pups seemed impervious to the atmosphere, but Star was even more subdued, going anxiously from one person to the other, looking for a normal reaction. Even Rab and Meg were bothered.

Jamie phoned early in the evening, hoping to give some comfort, though he knew there was little he could do. It would take time.

Shelley refused to speak to him.

'There's nothing we can do,' Sheina said, when he protested.

Jamie, who had just put a very old dog to sleep and tried, in vain, to stem the owner's tears, had nothing to say in answer. He hung up. He longed to go to Shelley. He wished she would let him share more of her life . . . all of her life.

Greg and Sheina kept Dannie busy during the day feeding the chickens and calves and ducks and collecting the eggs. He was silent and sullen and ready to shout at them if any tiny thing annoyed him. Greg decided they would tidy one of the sheds, as much to distract himself as Dannie.

Greg too had thought of buying the pups. But suppose the Greys didn't want to sell Amber and Hero? He was prepared to pay a fair price. Jamie had looked up the breed on the internet. Golden Retriever pups sold for as much as five hundred pounds each.

It would help them if they could keep them. They were as much part of the family as Star. Star could not be replaced. Greg could not settle and that night he took Rab out and walked on the hills, returning at midnight exhausted but still angry at the hand that fate had dealt them.

Sheina, worried about all of them, gave up trying to relax and made a huge batch of pies and pasties to put in the freezer for days when there was no time to cook. She could not go to bed until Greg came home. He said nothing when he did return. He dried Rab and hung up his wet clothes and went off to bed.

Shelley couldn't sleep either. Her thoughts whirled. She did not call Star but the dog sensed her unhappiness and came to curl up on the armchair beside the bed, her head on Shelley's shoulder. It made matters worse.

Thursday came too soon. Sheina was up early. She helped Shelley dress, knowing she would be better working than lying waiting and brooding. There were no guests until Matt and Liz came. Star helped, knowing the routine. The last time, Shelley thought, fighting tears again. Her throat ached.

A cold nose pushed into her hand, but today that was no help at all. Dannie plodded into the kitchen, still in his pyjamas, hair rumpled. He looked at Shelley and said nothing. He opened the back door and let Star into the yard. The other dogs were already outside and she greeted them and then indulged in one of their wild romps. She ended after only a few minutes, and came indoors again, worried by the family's strange behaviour.

Greg looked at his grandson.

'You'll have to look sharp to get ready for school,' he said. 'Shall I help you?'

'Not going to school. They'll take our dogs away while I'm there.'

'They won't even arrive till you get home,' Greg said. 'They've a very long journey. I promise she'll still be here.'

He sympathized with Dannie, but it would be better for the child to be occupied than to stay at home all day and fret. Jamie was busy calving a reluctant cow and had phoned to say he wouldn't be over to drive Dannie to meet the school bus.

Greg distracted his grandson by pretending the car wouldn't start, so they travelled the mile to the bus stop in the tractor. It was a slow journey, and Greg was afraid they might not make it in time. Dannie was always pestering Greg to take him into the cab. Greg felt small boys and tractors didn't mix. But just this once . . .

Excited voices greeted the child as he climbed on to the bus. A ride in a tractor . . . cool!

Jamie called in briefly just after lunch, but did not go indoors. Greg was in the big barn. He needed a major occupation to drown his thoughts. He was trying to restore it to order. Shelley had suggested they started a farm museum, and there were many useful objects. He was looking with some bemusement at a paraffin-heated incubator he had just discovered tucked away behind a broken plough and a small pile of tractor parts.

He looked up as Jamie came in, and left the incubator. Sheina bought the inevitable mugs of coffee and they sat on the low wall just outside the barn.

'There's lots of good stuff in here,' he said. 'You just put

160

things away when they cease to work and then forget them. That incubator has some mileage. My father used it to hatch out rare birds. It has the advantage of being immune to power cuts. I might start doing that again. A new interest for Shelley.'

'Good idea. She'll need one. I've tried to find her a trained dog, but there isn't one anywhere. I put her on the waiting list. But it won't be Star.'

Jamie picked up a round mottled pebble from the ground and turned it over and over in his hands, staring at it as if hoping it held the answers to all their problems.

'I went to the police station yesterday. Somewhere out there, Andy Scott reckons, is a farm that's harbouring the villains who took Star. He's discovered that there are several gangs stealing bitches in whelp or with their pups. It's usually easy as the owners aren't suspicious and don't have state-of-the-art precautions against theft. At least, not till it's happened, and then it's stable door mentality.'

Andy Scott was their village constable.

'We reckon that Star wouldn't have roamed very far from their base, especially as she was almost ready to whelp. She must have escaped. They're working on a thirty-mile circle with the farm as the centre.'

Greg thought back.

'I was probably about three quarters of a mile from home when I found her.'

'It would be a major advantage to find the villains and put paid to their activities,' Jamie said. 'It's too easy . . . fast travelling along the motorways, and finish up miles away from the place they come from. Sell the dogs in the pub. If they're a long way from home nobody will recognize them. There are several old farms across the valley where the folk keep to themselves and we don't know them. They have been bought by incomers.'

Greg's thoughts were still with Shelley and Dannie.

'I'm hoping the Greys'll sell me Amber and Hero. That would help a little, especially with Dannie. He had such high hopes and he's been doing so well. I wish now we'd tried to train Amber the way Star's trained, but there's never been enough time.'

Star trotted across the yard, a mobile phone in her mouth.

Shelley was in her room and Sheina in the shop. The call was for Jamie. A valuable stallion had jumped barbed wire in the hope of reaching a mare on the next farm. He had done a lot of damage to himself and would need a great deal of stitching.

Greg went back to exploring the contents of the barn, but his mind was still on the future. Star and her two pups were part of the family. Losing them would be like an amputation.

Sheina spent her spare time wondering about Star's first owners. What kind of people were they? They obviously had cared a great deal for their dog. They sounded so excited when they booked their rooms, asking after Star and whether she was well. They would be here all too soon.

She went out to pick flowers from her tiny garden and arrange them in a vase in their bedroom. If she kept busy she would not spend her time worrying about the days to come.

She decided that she and Shelley would spend the afternoon making an inventory of everything in the farm shop and plan new lines to sell. It was a taxing task and would leave little time for thought.

Jamie wanted to be there when Star's owners arrived. He hoped that his presence would help. His father agreed to take evening surgery, leaving him free.

He arrived at the farm almost at the same moment as Matt and Liz who drove in behind him. Dannie was standing in the back doorway, holding Star by the collar. She did not recognize Matt's new car.

Matt opened the door and sat, unbelieving, looking at the dog. There was no doubt at all. This was Star. At the same moment she caught his scent, and, pulling herself free, raced to him, greeting him with every fibre of her body. She rippled all over. Every part of her body waved as well as her tail. She moaned softly, an extraordinary sound that seemed an agony of delight. She rolled over, four paws in the air, tongue hanging out, asking for a tummy rub.

He knelt beside the dog, holding her. That was how she had always greeted him after an absence. He had a lump in his throat and hid his face from the bystanders. The dog

162

licked his face. Liz caught her breath. This was indeed Star. She watched, sudden tears in her eyes.

Jamie went in to find Shelley, who was with Greg and Sheina watching through the window. Shelley said nothing. Her last hope had gone. She turned her chair and wheeled it into her bedroom and shut the door. Her parents walked out into the yard. Jamie hesitated, wondering whether to knock on her door. There was no doubt whatever that Star belonged to the Greys.

'I can't believe it,' Matt said, standing up.

Star had exhausted her welcome. She sat in front of him, staring up at him, leaning against his legs. Matt had come at last.

A moment later he was startled to be attacked by a small whirlwind, shouting at him, pummelling him, crying.

'You can't take her away. You can't have her. She's ours now. She's been ours for years and years and years and she's not yours any more.'

Jamie reached Dannie before his grandfather could and lifted him. Dannie's fury turned on to the vet and his small fists went on hitting.

'Take him into the house,' Greg said softly. 'He'll upset Shelley even more.'

Jamie went into the kitchen to try and soothe the child, although he knew there was nothing whatever that would console him. Greg walked over to Matt and Liz who were standing, shaken.

'I'm so sorry,' he said.

He guessed there was no need to explain.

Matt looked at him, his pleasure dimmed and almost extinguished.

'I should have thought,' he said. 'We were so delighted to find she was alive and safe and well. Della didn't tell me you had a child.'

Greg could think of nothing to say. He led the way to their suite. Star, unaware of the pain she was causing, followed.

Greg left them. There was no doubt about the fervour with which she had greeted her former owner. Star was already lost to them.

Nineteen

Star followed Matt and Liz upstairs, and settled on the hearthrug in the little sitting room. It felt as if she had never been away from them. Matt looked at her. She had matured in the years since he lost her. Her coat was a richer gold than he remembered and was thick and wavy.

'Oh, Star,' he said, and her tail waved in ecstasy.

'They adore her,' Liz said.

Half his pleasure was dimmed.

Neither of them had thought of anything but being reunited with the dog that had been a vital part of their lives for nearly two years.

Liz was choked with tears. She wanted to go to Dannie and hold him tight and wipe away the hurt. They had been so happy at the thought of seeing Star again. They had not stopped to think about her new home, or how those there would feel about her.

Shelley stayed in her room. She could not face meeting them and they were unaware of her existence. Della had told them nothing about their hosts. She had been so excited at finding Star alive and well. They did not live near enough to the Greys to visit: their home was on the East coast of England, near Ipswich.

They were what Liz termed Christmas card friends. She now wished that she had asked more about their hosts. Like Della and Paul, they had been excited by the news that Star was alive and well. It had not occurred to them to wonder much about her new home. Star was lying on the rug in their sitting room, though her ears listened for Shelley's voice.

There was a notice pinned to the wall, giving the times of meals. They could take their meals, if they wished, with the family. The brochure said 'Bed and breakfast. Or full board with farmhouse meals a speciality.'

The rooms were well furnished and comfortable, with picture windows looking out on to the hills. Far away, the setting sun was reflected on a little loch. Matt looked at it without seeing it. All he saw was a distraught small boy about to lose his dog.

'Do you still think they stole her?' Liz asked.

'They don't seem the type. But how did they know her name?'

They went downstairs, Star shadowing them. There was no one in the kitchen, which was where Sheina had said they would eat, unless they preferred to have their meal alone, served in the dining room. The big table was already set for a meal.

They wanted to get to know their hosts. To find out more about Star and how she had come to be with them.

'Smells good,' Matt said, aware of the rich tantalizing smell of cooking food.

It was a moment before he realized the dog had a problem. She wanted to stay with him, but she had her own routine. She was part of Shelley's daily life and much of it was done at certain times. She knew the times as well as Shelley and Dannie.

She nosed Matt's leg and looked up at him, as if explaining she had other commitments now.

Her dilemma was solved. The phone rang. Star knew her duty. She turned at once, trotted across the floor and took it from the stand.

Shelley was still in her room. She had closed the door to keep the dog out. Her presence was a constant reminder of their imminent loss. Star could not reach her, so she offered the phone to Matt. He looked down at her, amazed that she still remembered. Had they discovered her skills and were using her as she had been trained?

He went to the outer door and called out. When Greg came in, Matt handed him the phone.

'That was one of the first things I taught her,' he said.

Greg answered the phone.

'For you,' he said, handing it to Jamie, who took it outside into the yard.

'Is the small boy your son?' Matt asked Sheina.

Dannie had been sent to wash his hands.

'Grandson,' she answered. She realized that they had not yet seen Shelley. 'He and his mother live with us. His father was killed in a car crash two years ago, and his mother was so badly injured she's in a wheelchair. Star's been invaluable.'

That information made Matt feel even worse.

Star settled herself beside his chair.

He looked at her two pups, now well grown. They must be nearly two years old. He found it hard to believe that Star had been missing all that time.

'We called them Amber and Hero,' Greg said. 'Dannie named them.'

Sheina handed round plates on which were slices of beef. Golden roast potatoes were flanked by carrots and peas and broccoli. The tiny Yorkshire puddings were feather light.

She passed them a small bowl.

'Watch the horseradish. It's home grown and it's very hot.'

Jamie came through the door.

'Stay and eat with us,' Sheina said when she saw him.

Jamie took a chair.

'That phone call was Andy. He's our local constable,' he explained to the Greys. 'They began enquiries when they discovered where Star came from. They've found out where she was taken. It's a farmhouse about thirty miles from here, which was left by an uncle to his nephew ten years ago. They don't farm. The fields are now waste ground.'

He looked up as Dannie came back into the room and nodded to the chair beside him. Greg prayed the child would behave.

Matt put down his knife and fork. The news was some consolation.

'Everyone thought it was a normal breeding kennels. There's one man there all the time, looking after the bitches, after a fashion. They breed them every six months, and discard them as worn out when they've had around eight litters. The place is a slum. They've found eight bitches, some with pups and some near to whelping. The police are trying to trace their owners.'

166

'Have they found the men who took them?' Matt asked, his mind on vengeance. He no longer suspected Greg. He hoped the villains would suffer a long prison sentence.

'They're due back tonight, according to the man who lives there. They'll get a surprise, as he's at the police station and the police are in the house waiting for them. The RSPCA have taken the dogs. The police now know all about Star. That's what triggered the investigation.'

Jamie grinned.

'Andy asked about her and she's well remembered. Apparently she recovered from doping when she was in the van and leaped out and bit the man trying to get her out, and then ran off. He needed eight stitches, they were told. I hope he suffered.'

'They half wrecked our house,' Matt said. 'They took all my trophies . . . my memories. Not one was left. They tore up the rosettes.'

'Trophies?' Greg looked across at him with sudden recognition. Matt Grey. 'Matthew Grey . . . you won the sheepdog trials. In 1995. Wales, wasn't it? I travelled in those days. Life was very different then. I was third that year. You had a good dog.'

'Boss. Short for Bossyboots.' He laughed. 'That was a pup and a half. Really sorted me out when I tried to train him. He had his own mind and that cost me places. But that year he really got his act together.'

'You still farm?' He passed the cream jug, while Sheina cut slices of lemon meringue pie.

'Sold up after we lost Star,' Matt said.

'What made you train her as you did?'

Matt laughed.

'She did. She carried everything she could pick up so we decided it would be a good idea to teach her to bring things to us, rather than run off with them and bury them, and then dig them up again and bring them in dirty and stuff them behind the cushions on the settee.'

'One day she hid a dead mouse that one of the cats had caught. She was an imp when she was a pup,' Liz said. 'We had such fun with her.'

Matt had another thought in his mind.

167

'How on earth did you know her name was Star?'

'She told us,' Jamie said. 'When she began to bring us things we needed, I said "what a star," and she went crazy, obviously recognizing the word, so we thought that must have been her name.'

It was such a simple explanation.

'That's how she came by her name with us,' Matt said. 'She is a star. It's wonderful to find her safe and so well. She looks magnificent, and so do the pups. Were there only two?'

'I did find one frozen on the hillside,' Greg said. 'I would think there were more, but she had been living wild for at least six weeks, having to forage for herself. It was very cold while she was out there. When the pups were tiny they'd be targets for owls, and hawks, and there's a pair of eagles up on the tops. She'd have had to leave them to find food.'

'I wonder how she escaped?' Liz said. 'She must have been so terrified. Do they know anything much about the men who took her?'

'There are four of them,' Jamie said. 'The one who stays here and three who go hunting for in-whelp bitches. Two grown men and a teenager, who is apparently only half in this world as he's a drug addict and they think he's also mentally disturbed. The barns are full of stolen property. They flog what they can but have all sorts of things they can't sell. There's a load of silver cups, and salvers and such, all engraved, belonging to various people. Apparently the teenager could never resist them. Goes for things that glitter.'

Matt wondered if they would get their treasured possessions back. The thieves had ransacked the house. All Liz's jewellery, most of it of sentimental value, inherited from her mother and aunts, had been taken. All his cups and salvers.

Jamie looked at Shelley's empty space at the table.

'Shelley not joining us?'

'She didn't feel up to it,' Greg said.

Jamie took a tray and Sheina dished up a plate of food for her daughter. Jamie added his cup of coffee. Dannie had eaten part of his meal and vanished.

Jamie turned before picking up the tray and looked at Matt.

'I think, if you don't mind, it would be better if you took

Star and her pups very early tomorrow. Perhaps you can find somewhere else to stay for the rest of your visit. The sooner they're gone the sooner Dannie and Shelley will settle. It would be agony for them to have her here another day, knowing they'll never see her again.'

He went out, shutting the door in what was almost a slam.

Matt looked down at his plate. The food had lost all flavour. Jamie might as well have said 'I wish you'd never come.'

The family spent the evening watching television without taking in any of it. There was nothing to say. Star had left Shelley and was once more with Liz and Matt. Greg, watching the dog, thought that she did not know where she belonged now. She looked back at him before she followed them, as if unsure of her role.

She'd go back to a familiar place with people she knew well and would soon settle. He wondered how soon they would all recover. Star would leave a bigger gap than any dog he had ever owned. He had never trained a dog the way that she was trained. Perhaps Matt would give him some pointers.

Sheepdogs were easy to train as they had the need within them, and he had always had dogs with strong herding drives. Star's skills were so different. The pups seemed to have inherited some of her ability. Perhaps, trained properly, they would show more. Amber was biddable but Hero was stubborn, with a mind of his own, and his adolescent months had been far from easy.

He had taught Dannie a great deal.

Matt had many questions, needing to know more about Star's first months with them. By bedtime Greg knew all about Star's first two years, and Matt and Liz knew how she had spent the last two. They all wondered how she had spent the weeks living wild. It was an uneasy evening, with Star commuting between Shelley and the Greys, as if unable to make her mind up just where she belonged.

Bedtime was even worse. Matt suggested that the dog should choose where she slept. She hesitated as he and Liz went towards the staircase. Shelley's rooms were all on the ground floor. Dannie had fallen asleep on the settee, and

Sheina had not had the heart to send him to his empty room. The dog's rug was still between the two rooms, at the side of the connecting doorway.

Star made up her mind. Her bed for the past two years had been in the doorway between Dannie and Shelley and that was where she now belonged. She looked up at Matt, as if trying to explain. After a minute, she trotted to her usual sleeping place. Greg carried Dannie through to his bed. He woke and saw Star and welcomed her, disbelieving. After Greg had gone he again left his bed and curled up on her rug on the floor, his head against her shoulder, his duvet over both of them.

Tomorrow night she would be gone. Maybe Grandad would buy him a new dog to sleep near his bed, but it wouldn't be the same. He cried until he was exhausted and then fell asleep, holding her tightly, his face buried in her fur.

He was the only one who slept. Shelley felt bleak. She had no more tears to shed, just an aching misery that coloured everything grey. Greg and Sheina both lay awake, worrying.

'Funny,' Sheina said, wondering if the night would ever pass. 'You think when they're grown up they'll be off your hands and life will be worry free, at least as far as your children are concerned. It just gets worse.'

Greg sighed.

'Cut knees and failed exams and measles are much easier, though you don't realize it at the time,' he said.

Matt and Liz were silent as they undressed, neither wishing to share their thoughts. Matt looked out of the window at the floodlit farmyard and watched the dogs let out for their last run. Even they seemed subdued.

He slept fitfully and woke, as always, at four thirty. That was a habit he seemed unable to break. Milking time. He had loved his cow herd. He felt a sudden pang. He missed his animals. He was now on familiar ground, but there was no herd here. Only Toffee.

He dressed and went outside. Dawn flooded the mountains with scarlet. The sky was streaked with black clouds and a niggling wind that promised a rainy day.

Shepherd's warning. Those old rhymes were so often right. He walked out of the farmyard on to the moors. He wished he had thought to ask more about Star's new family before they came. He had not yet met Shelley.

He walked down to the little loch and stood, staring at the water, as if it could supply the answer to his problems. Wind ruffled the surface, covering it with flecks of white. An osprey dived and surfaced with a trout almost too big for him to hold. He thumped its head against the rock until its struggles were stilled and then began to eat.

Matt returned at breakfast time. Star was in the yard and ran to greet him. He knelt beside her, holding her, wishing life had been different, cursing the men who had ruined their lives. Star leaned against him. She had not yet been fed. Sheina was putting down her meal for the last time. It was time to eat. Star left him and ran over to the open kitchen door and went inside.

Sheina cooked bacon and eggs, black pudding, mushrooms and fried bread, tomatoes and sausages. It was a rare treat. At home breakfast was a quick meal of cereal and toast.

When they'd eaten Matt went out into the yard, Greg following him, determined to ask if he would sell the two pups. Dannie had gone to school and made Greg promise he would not let her owners take Star while he was away.

'He can't come back to an empty house,' Greg said when Sheina protested, sure it would be better if Matt and Liz went while the child was away.

'I'd like to buy the two pups,' he said as he stood in the yard with Matt watching them play. Both men were uneasy. Matt felt almost as if he were the thief, taking the dog from her owners.

Greg tried to explain.

'It would help Dannie. He regards them as his. He's been training Hero for Obedience. There's a big show this month. They've entered. Maybe I could teach Amber to do all that Star does for Shelley.'

Greg hoped that his request would be granted and not be taken amiss. Dannie had been so much happier this past two years and owed much of that to the dogs. As for Shelley . . . he doubted if Amber could make up for Star.

'I'll pay you their full value.'

'They must have cost you to keep all this time,' Matt said.

'I'd be delighted to leave them here. I don't want money for them. I never thought to see them again. Star isn't too old to have another litter.'

He was about to say more, but they were now outside Shelley's room. They could see her sitting in her chair, her back to the window, Star beside her. It was their special time. Star seemed to have a clock inside her head. She approached Shelley, a length of twisted coloured rope in her mouth. Shelley was almost in tears.

She didn't want even to try but Star persisted, pushing the rope at her over and over until at last she gave in. The last time. She took the end and Star tugged.

The tug pulled Shelley to her feet. Shelley stood in front of her chair. She was making a tremendous effort and did not see the watchers.

Then she released the rope and, holding on to the arms of the chair, she collapsed into it. It was a clumsy, uncoordinated movement, as she had not managed to take all her weight and lower herself gently.

The effort exhausted her. Her unhappiness overwhelmed her.

Star put her front paws on Shelley's knees. Shelley leaned forward and held the dog tight, savouring her, unable to see for tears.

Star was not satisfied. She thrust the rope again at Shelley. This time, when Shelley took it, Star, instead of standing still, walked backwards, still tugging. Shelley stood again, and managed to move one foot forward. Then her courage deserted her. The second leg refused to move at all. Her back was hurting.

She made another effort, but the will had gone. She stood briefly but lost her balance and fell into the chair instead of lowering herself carefully. She had not done that for some weeks. Without Star she could not continue to progress. The dog forced her to try. The tugging made an enormous difference, and enabled her to use the dog's strength to help her stand. She hated anyone but Star watching her efforts.

Neither man had noticed that Liz and Sheina were standing behind them.

'I didn't know she could do that,' Sheina said.

172

Star was determined. Shelley stood again but this time she could not move even one step. She ached all over from the effort. She needed to rest. Maybe later . . . and then she realized there would be no later. This time was the last.

Matt turned away and looked at the mountains, asking for strength of mind. He had no choice.

'We can't take Star,' he said. 'Shelley needs her more than we do. She might fret for me for a day or two, but she belongs here. Don't you agree?' he asked, turning to Liz.

Liz nodded. She had come, very reluctantly, to the same conclusion.

'Just one thing,' Matt said. 'If she does have another litter, may we have a pup?'

Sheina stared and then hugged Matt, unable to speak.

'We'll send you her papers, and you can change her ownership,' Matt said, and felt a sudden lifting of his spirits as he spoke. 'Let's tell Shelley.'

Greg knocked on the door before opening it, and led Matt and Liz in. Shelley stared at them, suddenly angry. She had no desire at all to welcome Star's real owners. What on earth possessed her father to bring them in to introduce them?

Matt guessed her distress.

'We aren't taking Star,' he said. 'You need her more than we do. We taught her for fun. She asked for it, and was so clever. I never dreamed she could do so much for anyone like you. We'd just like one of her pups if you have a litter from her next year. We'll send you her papers.'

The joy in Shelley's eyes was reward enough. Matt felt as if an enormous burden had been lifted from him. He could never have lived with Star, knowing how much she was missed.

Greg rang Jamie, who picked Dannie up from school, instead of from the bus stop, telling him the news as soon as he saw him. Dannie's eyes glistened with excitement.

'It's really really really true?' he asked over and over again. 'You're not just pretending?'

'Really true,' Jamie assured him.

Dannie couldn't wait to get home. He jumped out of the car as soon as they reached the yard, calling for Star, who ran to him and greeted him, overjoyed to see him again. She was as excited as he, aware of a difference in the atmosphere of the house. She ran beside him as he raced inside to see his mother.

Matt and Liz were with Shelley. Dannie stopped in the doorway and stared and then flung himself at Matt.

'I'm sorry I said I hated you,' he said. 'I love you. Thank you a zillion zillion. I thought I'd never see Star again.'

Matt knew he would never forget Star, but he had made a new life since she went, and if he had one of her pups to remember her by, he would be well content.

Jamie came over again in the evening after surgery, to share in a feast that Shelley cooked for all of them. When the meal was over Shelley looked at Matt and Liz.

They could not believe the difference in her. The colour had come back into her face and she glowed with happiness.

'I can't thank you enough,' she said. 'Star saved my sanity. She gave me a reason for living again.'

She did not know that her efforts that afternoon had been watched. She wondered whether to show them what Star could do for her and then changed her mind. It would remain a secret until, one day, she would walk across the room unaided, surprising everyone.

Shelley smiled at them, her face alive with joy.

'She's made so much difference to our lives,' she said. 'When Dad found her I thought I'd never be happy again. I can't tell you what she's done for me.'

They left next morning.

'We'll keep in touch,' Greg said, before they waved goodbye. 'And we won't forget that pup next year.'

Star watched them go from the window, Shelley in her wheelchair beside the dog. Dannie had said goodbye before he went to school and the sight of his jubilant face and beaming smile and fervent kiss stayed with the Greys for the journey home.

Star watched them drive away. For a couple of days she seemed subdued, but then she recovered her joy in living, and she and Dannie played excited games. He put all his energy into training Hero.

Jamie thought the child would burst with excitement on the day of the show. They came home late, Dannie asleep, but he woke up as they drove into the yard.

He raced into the kitchen waving a yellow rosette.

'We came fourth. The judge said it was very good for a first time at a big show and one day Hero will win. And everyone else was older than me. And when I'm older I'll be the best. We stopped for fish and chips on the way home and Jamie says he'll take me to more big shows next year.'

Jamie laughed.

'We'll need to keep this one from being cock of the walk,' he said.

'Be easy.' Greg put the rosette up with the others that Dannie had won. 'Next time out, he probably won't come anywhere. Keep his feet on the ground. Meanwhile let him enjoy a day of having his head in the clouds.'

His words added to Dannie's conviction that grownups were very odd indeed and said the most peculiar things.

Matt kept his promise to keep in touch. His long phone calls and reminiscences of Star's puppyhood helped to train Amber. Star needed no training. She watched, and discovered for herself what she could do to improve life for those around her.

Matt never tired of hearing about her progress.

Just after Christmas Greg was able to tell the Greys that the men who stole Star were now in jail and at least one gang who stole bitches had been stopped. Matt had his own news as the police brought back his stolen trophies. He could never replace the rosettes but the cups and salvers were engraved with his name, and once more took their place in the display cabinet in their sitting room.

That summer Star was mated again to the Manville dog. Jamie took her, Dannie going with him. Matt and Liz waited for the pups to be born as impatiently as those on the farm, praying that the whelping would be trouble-free and the litter healthy. You never knew what was in store.

Dannie rang the Greys in the middle of July.

'Star's got nine puppies, six girls and three boys. They're wonderful. Grandad says he'll pick a special one for you. He says when you come to get her we'll have a special celebration 'cos you let us keep her.'

He was so excited and speaking so fast that Liz found it difficult to understand him.

'Me and Hero . . . we came second last week in Dundee. Jamie says it's only a matter of time and we'll be first.'

Shelley took the phone from him.

'Star's loving all the attention. She shows her pups to everyone. She's a wonderful mother. It's too early to see which is going to the brightest. We're not letting anyone choose yet. We want the best for you.'

'I hope Lisa doesn't get jealous when we bring the pup home,' Liz said as she rang off. She smiled, as their dog, hearing her name, walked across the room to be petted. 'They're all so excited. We'd never have felt happy if we'd brought Star home. Shelley's come alive.'

Star was making up for everything she had missed with her first litter. She was obsessed by the pups at first, checking on them constantly after she had been away for a few minutes. She only made brief sorties during the first three weeks, as if afraid that someone might take her babies from her.

'She'll wash them away,' Dannie said, laughing, as her busy tongue licked them devotedly, making sure they were all clean. He was enthralled and spent most of his spare time watching them. He was now used to lambs and kids and calves but puppies were new to him.

Once they began to toddle, Star returned to her duties. Shelley had not missed her skills too much, as she was now able to do more for herself. Amber was nearly as good as her mother, and happy to take her place as Shelley's helper. Shelley spent almost as much time with the pups as Dannie.

Star seemed to want to share her babysitting duties.

'I think Heaven must a place where there are always puppies to cuddle,' Shelley said when Star unceremoniously dumped one of the little bitch pups in her lap during lunch. 'Is she asking me to share her responsibilities or does she think I need one of them to comfort me while she's busy with the rest of them?'

'They'll be too big for her to carry soon,' Greg said. 'I wonder what she'll do then?'

He soon found out. Star trotted over to Shelley, her pups trailing behind her. One after another tried to clamber on to Shelley's lap, as that was a place they already knew.

'Does she think I'm a dog? Or is she sure she's actually

human?' Shelley asked, laughing at the sprawl of tiny animals around her. Her chair seemed to be a focus when they were indoors. Sheina had carpeted the kitchen floor with thick layers of newspaper.

Once the pups were three weeks old, visitors were allowed to see them and play with them. There was no shortage of people to help them gain confidence. They could have sold the litter twice over, but Greg kept his promise. He wanted to make sure that Matt and Liz got the best of them.

They were soon bold little animals, racing for affection and cuddling, afraid of nothing. Sheina scattered the floor with toys. Dannie and Jamie visited a car boot sale and came back with an assortment of soft furry animals, all bought for fifty pence each. Visitors were entertained when met by a small determined pup bearing a knitted tortoise, or a battered teddy bear, or even a furry miniature giraffe in its mouth. Occasionally two pups argued over one toy. Star removed it from the squabblers, and took it away and hid it.

'I've never wasted so much time in my life,' Shelley said one afternoon when Dannie arrived home from school. 'I had no idea it was so late. I haven't even started tea.'

'Doesn't matter,' Dannie said. 'I want to play with the puppies.'

Greg had told him what to watch for. They hoped that all the litter would be good but that there would be one who was another Star. Each pup was marked by a dash of red nail varnish on one of its claws so that they could tell the difference between them, as at first they were all so alike in appearance.

By the time they began to develop character, everyone thought it obvious which one would be for Matt. Dannie christened her Comet.

Matt approved of the name when told.

'Maybe she'll shoot into history,' he said.

From the time she could first toddle, Comet loved to pick up anything that was small enough to get in her mouth. As well as soft toys, Sheina gave them an array of twists of rope, old socks, two discarded soft suede purses, very much the worse for wear, and an assortment of Dannie's outgrown trainers.

Comet not only played with them, but learned very fast that Dannie would play too, and she offered her trophies to him, sure they were wanted. Then she realized that the game could be much more fun as, when she brought them, Dannie threw them and she trotted after them, unsteadily at first but soon gaining confidence, and brought them back.

The other pups carried toys around, but none so frequently or so persistently as little Comet. They never brought them back to anyone, but trotted off with them to a corner, often falling asleep with their heads on their trophies.

The Greys had almost daily reports, but found time passed slowly. They booked in for a week, to get to know their pup before they took her home.

'I can't wait,' Matt said, a few days before they left for their visit. 'I've never known time go so slowly. I wonder what we are going to discover in the years to come. Little Comet might be a bigger star than her mother.'

At last the day of their journey arrived. Lisa was to come too, so that she could meet the little animal that was now to share her life. They arrived just after Dannie came home from school. He ran to greet them.

'All the other pups have gone to their new homes,' he said. 'There's just Comet now. Come and see her.'

Star came to meet them, her tail waving, a diminutive Comet trotting beside her. She greeted Matt sedately, welcoming him as a visitor to her life, but aware that this was where she now belonged. Liz brought Lisa out of the car, on her lead, and the two older dogs met, sniffing one another warily.

The pup, aware that this was just another Retriever like her mother, came up too, expecting to be greeted with pleasure. Lisa was suspicious, but within ten minutes the three were lying together in the kitchen, the pup alternately tweaking first her mother's tail and then the newcomer's.

Dannie threw a soft ball and the pup ran to it, picked it up and brought it to him.

'Wow!' Matt said. 'Another Star.'

He called softly.

'Hey, pup. Puppy, puppy, puppy.'

Comet eyed this new person with interest, then, deciding

he was worth investigating, picked up a toy dog that was bigger than she was and dragged it determinedly to his feet, where she sat beside it, looking up at him.

Matt laughed at her. She was used to people who laughed. Usually afterwards they cuddled her and she loved that too. She put her front paws against his legs, asking to be noticed. He lifted her and was rewarded with a licked nose and nibble at his ear.

Shelley came into the kitchen in her wheelchair. She greeted them happily, delighted to see them and also delighted that they had produced a perfect puppy for them.

She was looking well, and had put on weight. Star walked over to her, looking up at her as if asking if she were needed.

Matt glanced across at his wife. They had both hoped to see Shelley walking by now, even if on crutches. It was a disappointment, but maybe she would, one day, be free of the chair. Shelley was watching the pup, who was cuddled against Matt, as if she knew that was where she belonged.

'Like her?' she asked.

'I've already fallen in love,' Matt said.

'She's adorable.' Liz lifted the pup off Matt's lap and Comet snuggled against her shoulder. People, she already knew, were there entirely for her benefit.

Dannie was unable to settle. Excitement mastered him and he seemed to be unable to sit still. He grabbed Matt's hand.

'We've done lots since you were here,' he said. 'Come and see while Mum gets supper.'

Liz put the pup down beside her mother and followed them. She had forgotten how fast children grew. This sturdy boy was nothing like the child she remembered. He whistled to Hero who came at once.

'He's doing well,' Dannie said. 'We keep coming second. One day we'll be first.'

He led them across the yard. There was a new bungalow on the far side, its roof almost complete.

'That's for us. Mum and me and the dogs. It's going to be ready by Christmas. And this is the farm museum. It's in the big barn. Do you know when I was little I thought there was a ghost there? And it was only owls.'

The big barn was transformed, the walls whitewashed, the

179

array of long-abandoned machines and implements ranged neatly and labelled.

'This is my favourite,' Dannie said, leading them over to the paraffin-fuelled incubator. 'It still works though it's a bit smelly, and it's full of eggs from all sorts of birds. People bring them here for Mum to look after and hatch. We couldn't do it before 'cos when the weather's bad we get power cuts, and then the little birds inside the eggs die 'cos they get cold. With this, power cuts don't matter.'

'I thought you had a generator,' Matt said.

'We do, but it's not able to run everything. Grandad keeps it for lights and fridges and freezers and any machines he needs, and heaters. The house gets jolly cold if the central heating goes off. It would take too much power to run an incubator.'

'What kind of birds?' Matt asked, intrigued.

'We've had parrots and cockatiels and an osprey egg, and two peregrine eggs. The mother bird was poisoned, and the wardens brought them to us. They hatched out and now they're being looked after till they can be set free.'

Greg whistled across the yard.

'Time to eat.'

The dogs settled on the rug. Little Comet had her own ideas and thought if people were eating she should too, but Star brought her back to the rug and kept a paw on her, preventing her from pestering the diners. She protested loudly, but then settled, her head on her mother's side, her eyes watching the moving hands that carried food to the mouths.

When the dishwasher was stacked Dannie made coffee. He was simmering with suppressed excitement. The Greys had arrived on the Friday night.

'No school tomorrow,' Dannie said, as he handed the cups round. 'It's going to be a special day, isn't it, Grandad?'

Greg laughed.

'Dannie can never keep a secret. Tomorrow we all go out and celebrate,' Greg said. 'I've booked us lunch at the Castle. It was a castle once, and now it's a first class hotel. Our way of saying thank you. We owe you so much . . . without Star . . .'

'Liz believes we have guardian angels,' Matt said. 'Ours

180

led us to Star. Your angel led to her theft, and then to you.'

'A guiding star,' Liz said. 'She was meant for you, from the first.'

'Have I got a guardian angel?' Dannie asked. 'I think I must have. Do you remember when I ran away and got locked in the tractor, Grandad? My guardian angel must have helped me then.'

He held out his plate for another roast potato, and his expression suddenly changed.

'But where was my dad's that night?'

It was not a question anyone could answer and a momentary shadow passed over them all.

'It'll be quite a party tomorrow,' Greg said, anxious for distraction. 'Jamie and his parents are coming too. It's a very splendid hotel so it's best dresses and suits for everyone.'

'What about the farm?' Matt asked.

'We've closed for the day. No visitors. Our neighbour Maggy's coming in so she can deal with anything that crops up. Angus has a locum for the next week, as Jamie is having time off. Hopefully nothing will go wrong.'

Dannie was bubbling with excitement, and reluctant to go to bed.

'He's never eaten out in a grand hotel before,' Sheina said, when at last he had been persuaded to leave the room. 'He can't wait for tomorrow.'

Shelley laughed.

'He keeps asking me if I'm sure he can have what we're having and not have to eat the children's menu. He's quite sure nine is really grown up, but afraid the waiter might not think so.'

'He has matured since we last saw him,' Matt said. 'He's a very nice boy. You should be proud of him.'

'I am,' Shelley said, as she wheeled herself out of the room.

Star followed her, and, as Comet was now alone, her last brother having gone to his new home that morning, the pup came too and settled beside her mother on the rug.

Next morning everyone helped with the chores, and then, after their coffee break, retired to dress for their outing. Dannie was first down, waiting impatiently for the adults.

181

'You look very smart,' Liz said, used to seeing him in jeans and T-shirt or sweater. He was wearing new trousers, and a shirt and tie under a dark jacket.

'I feel silly,' he said.

'You look wonderful,' Sheina said. 'Very handsome. All the girls will be breaking their hearts.'

Dannie gave her a disgusted look and she laughed.

'Come on, we're all going in my car. Grandad will bring Shelley as she needs more room than we do.'

The weather was kind, the sun shining, the sky blue with fragmented clouds. The lanes were still summer bright though there were signs of leaves turning to autumn flame. There was an early morning nip in the air that was soon dispelled by bright sunlight.

The Castle Hotel stood on a small hill just beyond the village. It had once been a grand house for grand people. Sheina often wondered how it felt to own such a place and live there with the huge staff that would be needed to run it.

And no electricity or running water, no machines to make life easy. She was suddenly glad that she had been born into the twentieth century and lived to see the twenty-first. So much had changed.

They drove round the edge of a loch whose dark waters were edged with white sand. A huge gate flanked by lions on pillars led into a sweeping drive bordering park-like lawns in which were beds bright with autumn flowers.

Dannie was wide eyed, overcome by such grandeur. He had never seen the hotel before.

'Wow. Those dahlias are as big as dinner plates. It's magic,' he said, looking at tables and chairs, sheltered by bright umbrellas, stood on a wide terrace, where Jamie and his parents waited for them. Large glass doors opened into a huge dining room, decorated with flowers, the tables laid for the midday meal.

Jamie fetched drinks for everyone, and a glass of home-made lemonade for Dannie.

'Grandad's late,' Dannie said. There were still times when he had a niggling fear that those he loved would have an accident and vanish for ever as his father had. He lay awake at night if any of his family went out, and could not go to sleep until he was sure that everyone was safely home.

'I expect it took time to get the wheelchair in the car,' Jamie said, aware of his worry.

Greg's car came to a halt on the drive.

He got out and waved to them. He opened the boot, removed the wheelchair and unfolded it, ready for Shelley. He then went to the back door of the car and opened it. Matt and Liz looked blankly at the woman who got out. She wore a gold dress and a matching hat that hid her face.

Greg looked at her, bemused, as she ignored his outstretched hand.

She stood quite still and then lifted her head.

Jamie stared at her.

Very slowly, she walked towards them. Before she had moved three steps, Star was beside her, her ears up, her body swaggering, her tail banner high and waving.

'Shelley!'

Everyone was incredulous.

Shelley removed her hat and smiled at them.

'I wanted to surprise you. If it hadn't been for Star . . . and you . . . I wouldn't be walking now.'

Jamie reached her first, hugging her, and then taking her arm to lead towards the steps.

'I can't believe it,' Liz said as she too ran down the steps and hugged Shelley. Matt joined them, and was hugged too.

Shelley laughed.

'I've been bursting to tell you all, but I didn't want to spoil it. Not even Jamie knew. He has a surprise announcement to make too.'

'You've given me an even bigger surprise,' he said. 'I wondered why you had changed your mind.'

He smiled at the faces watching him, wondering what he was about to say.

'We wanted you all here,' he said. 'But we had a secret. It's a special day. Not just a thank you for Star day. You've come to attend a wedding.'

'I said I wouldn't marry him until I could walk again,' Shelley said. 'We did it, didn't we, Star?'

Star's sudden joyous bark echoed in the hills as Jamie took Shelley's arm to help her up the steps into the hotel where the minister awaited them.

EM